MW01595699

JACK WILSON
Chief Petty Officer, U.S.N.

Joe Abate
Thanks for buying
my book. Hope
you enjoy it -

[signature]

JACK WILSON
Chief Petty Officer, U.S.N.

Leon R. Shafer

Pleasant W rd
A Division of WINEPRESS PUBLISHING

Printed in the United States of America

Packaged by Pleasant Word, a division of WinePress Publishing, PO Box 428, Enumclaw, WA 98022. The views expressed or implied in this work do not necessarily reflect those of Pleasant Word, a division of WinePress Publishing. Ultimate design, content, and editorial accuracy of this work are the responsibilities of the author.

ISBN 1-4141-0232-1
Library of Congress Catalog Card Number: 2004094793

Table of Contents

Chapter 1

It was in the spring of 1968 when I drove through the gate of the Naval Air Station, Alameda and went straight to the disbursing office. I stepped out of my new Buick and took in a deep breath.

It was the beginning of a beautiful day. I was running a little late and the sun was starting to peek over the mountains east of Oakland.

As I took in the air, I was glad the rains had stopped. It had been raining for the past couple days. I do mean rain. It wasn't one of the fog/smog drizzles that the bay area is noted for. This was a real rain, and the air was fresh and clean.

I went to the disbursing office to pick up my re-enlistment check. As I walked in the door, I said, "I'm Chief Wilson. I came in for my check."

I was answered, "Yeah, I know, Chief. I'm working on it. I'll have it ready in a minute."

"How about me using your phone?"

"Sure, Chief. Help yourself."

I called the Aviation Maintenance Department Electronics Shop. That's where I worked. I was the CPO in charge.

I called just to let them know where I am. I don't think anybody really cares. The Division Officer likes to know, but does he really care? No. Just as long as the work gets done and everything goes smoothly, the Maintenance Officer is satisfied, the Division Officer is satisfied, and of course, I'm satisfied.

After I finished my business at the disbursing office, I drove over to the shop. Everyone there had already received their paychecks.

This was payday for everyone. Most of the crew had gone out to the mobile check cashing van in front of the shop. Work is quite slack for the first few hours of the morning on payday.

I was sitting at my desk adding up my checks when the phone rang.

"Chief Wilson speaking, sir."

"Jack. This is Chief Michaels, personnel office. Your orders just came in."

This was it! The transfer orders I had been waiting for. Normal rotation for my rate of Aviation Electronics Technician Chief was three years shore duty and eighteen months sea duty. My three years of shore duty were coming to an end.

Some time back, I had talked with the Chief at the assignment desk in the Bureau of Personnel, Washington. I had been told I was to be assigned to the Naval Air Station, Atsugi, Japan. This was exactly what I wanted and asked for.

When Chief Michaels said "orders," I mentally started making travel arrangements for my wife, Doris, and myself. If everything went right, we could still make it to Japan during the spring. I was swept into my recollections of my previous springtime visits in Japan. The crisp of winter would still be in the air and the blossoms would soon be popping out on the trees. Everything was perfect to make an impressionable arrival. Doris would love it.

In my excitement, I stood as I continued my mental journey through some of the things that would have to be taken into account. We would need passports, shots, packing and, of course, transportation.

I was jolted back out of my dreams as he said, "Your orders are to the USS Kreighton."

When the Chief Personnelman said USS, my stomach drew up into a knot. I felt hot and cold flashes. I broke into a sweat.

Time stood still, yet, I could see the room begin to spin. Faster, faster, faster. My whole body went slack as the room spun away into the blackness of unconsciousness.

The boys Jack chummed around with during high school were up to something. Jack had no idea of what, but sensed he wanted no part of it.

Somehow, he knew whatever they were up to would end up destroying the property of some individual. After all, it was Halloween.

Nobody liked pranks more than Jack, but he couldn't see being destructive.

In Ottawa Kansas, teenagers had to create their own excitement or become absolutely bored stiff. He told them someday he would have his day. Pranks at the monetary expense of someone else just weren't his cup of tea.

"Jack, you're just too good hearted. You'll never pull off one as good as the one we have planned for tonight. Better come with us."

"No thanks," Jack said as the other guys went on their way to have their type of fun.

Only his daydreaming lowered Jack's grades throughout school. Daydreaming of travel, of success. He didn't want to make a big splash in the world. He just wanted to travel enough to become worldly educated. Success to him meant a significant achievement in the profession he would choose.

Jack was a good young man. The guys in his group had called him "good hearted." Yes, Jack was that and perhaps a little more. He enjoyed people. He enjoyed life. *Toujours Gai*-Always Happy. He had a good smile and a good word for everyone with whom he associated.

He worked part-time as an apprentice in the only print shop in town. He worked after school and during the summer vacation. He had worked for Mr. Johnston for over two years and became proficient in his work. He knew he didn't want to be stuck in Ottawa for the rest of his life.

The day the high school principal came into the print shop and talked with Mr. Johnston, he was excluded from the conversations. He had taken job orders from the principal before, but this time he insisted on speaking with Mr. Johnston in private.

After the principal left, Jack asked Mr. Johnston what it was all about. Why the secrecy? Had he done something he shouldn't have? Mr. Johnston assured him he had not done anything out of the way and that the conversation didn't pertain to him at all.

Of course, Mr. Johnston couldn't tell him what the conversation was about and this intensified Jack's curiosity. He just had to find out what it was.

What Jack's amateur sleuthing uncovered was Mr. Johnston was to print tickets for the senior graduation exercises. There were 500 seats in the high school auditorium, and the principal wanted only 388 tickets printed. No more!

This would give a seat to each graduating student and the tickets were for the remaining seats. They were to be distributed, one for each parent, one for each faculty member, and one for each invited dignitary.

There was no ticket system the previous year, and some uninvited guests appeared causing some faculty members, parents, or guests to stand. Slight that it was, the principal didn't want it to happen again.

When Jack received the two tickets for his parents, he immediately recognized the exact font. He knew the paper and ink also.

On his way to the print shop that afternoon, the idea struck him. Here was his opportunity. If everything went as he envisioned, he would receive the "Oscar of Pranks." That is, if such an award existed. He dwelled upon the scheme and concluded he wouldn't accept any credit for his anonymity would be paramount.

Mr. Mays, the editor of the local newspaper came into the print shop near the same time each day. He had completed his portion of the work and the printing of the paper was "their job" as he often phrased it. He would come in for a minute, and then he and Mr. Johnston would leave to discuss everything from world politics to the local topic of the day.

Whatever, they solved the problems of the world while they consumed from three to five cups of coffee.

Their absence was always a minimum of thirty minutes. Not only did Jack have this time, he had the hour or so after the shop closed for the day.

Mr. Johnston would call it a day and would leave the print shop shortly after 6 PM to go home. It was Jack's responsibility to lock the shop after his evening clean up. It was during these times that Jack created the vehicle of his master plan.

Absolute trust. It finally paid off!

Word sped throughout the community as to who was being invited to the exercises. This disturbed friends of the graduating class. It was a performance they couldn't attend. Had everyone been invited, they wouldn't have wanted to attend. Now that they were excluded, everyone seemed to want to be there.

On graduation night, there wasn't standing room in the auditorium. The hallways were packed with people trying to get in. There must have been a thousand people there. And, they all had tickets!

Jack had printed and distributed at least an additional 500 admission tickets.

As the graduation ceremonies were going on, the principal and faculty were frantic while Jack Wilson sat the lowest in his seat. His face bore the biggest smile, and he said to himself, "Here school. Here is your reward for my education."

"Welcome back. You've been smiling for sometime. What were you thinking about?" It was a womanish voice.

I looked around trying to grasp my unfamiliar surrounding. My search stopped when I saw Doris sitting in the chair beside my hospital bed. She related the events of the past thirty hours. A mild shock and acute gastric something or the other is what the doctor called it. My stomach had drawn up into a knot, and I was carried to sickbay as a ball of human flesh wrapped up in a Chief Petty Officers' uniform. After a few hours of trying to revive me or bring me back into the world of the living, the sickbay medics gave up.

While unconscious I was taken by ambulance to the naval hospital. The doctors assured Doris everything seemed to be all right. They told her for some reason I wanted to leave the world of reality so I had one long, deep sleep.

The hospital kept me overnight again. Their reason was to run a couple more tests. At first they thought I had a heart attack. I must have satisfied the doctors for they released me the next morning.

I called the Division Officer and told him I would like to take a couple of days off to think this mess over. This he granted without hesitation.

Something had happened to me, and no one seemed to know what. If the doctors didn't know what it was, then I wanted to know why. So, what it was didn't to seem to cross my mind too much. What I really wanted to know was why. I couldn't seem to think this thing out.

Doris picked me up at the hospital.

As she drove home, she related the experience of these past few days. I paid no attention to her words and just stared out the window of the car and even seemed to be unaware of the scenery as it passed by. I kept thinking of why this had such an effect on me. I just couldn't get things straight in my head.

In my naval career, I've had many disappointments. Failing examinations and not being promoted, passing examinations and not being promoted. These are only two, but they're the ones that would mean money in my pocket. Well, the money wasn't really that important; the successful achievements of desired goals were. Doris won enough golf tournaments to keep us in good money. I thought I deserved these promotions and that they were rightfully mine.

The money that these promotions would have brought would have been my contribution to the household. Her winnings are used for her golf expenses and what is left over, we put into the bank and into investments.

During my years in the U.S. Navy, I have been stationed in all parts of the United States. From San Diego,

California to Bremerton, Washington. From Jacksonville, Florida to Quonset Point, Rhode Island, and I'll swear all Naval Air Stations in between these four points. I've seen Panama and Trinidad in the Atlantic and most of the larger islands in the Pacific.

I've enjoyed this type of life and the people with whom I've worked. I've enjoyed my travels about the world and was impressed with the cultures and customs of the foreign countries I have visited.

I kept asking myself, "Why? Why did this have such an effect?" There must surely be a reason. The only logical conclusion I could come to was that I just didn't want to go to sea again. I didn't want to be aboard a ship as part of a crew and definitely not as "ships company."

If I must return to sea duty, let it be some place of my choice. I've never received orders of my choice since I enlisted almost eighteen years ago.

On my last "dream sheet" I requested orders to Atsugi, Sasebo, or Iwakuni, Japan. I even nailed down this dream sheet with what little influence I had as a friend of a friend. The last conversation I had with the Chief Petty Officer in charge of assignments for my rating at the assignment desk was that I would be going to Atsugi.

I loved my visits to Japan and had sold Doris on the idea of being stationed there. When I told her what I requested, she was thrilled with the thought of being stationed there. Over the years she had been quite a trooper. She would assist in making our travel arrangements, leave her friends, and make new ones. She would leave her golfing associates, her country clubs, and rebuild her social life again. She followed me everywhere.

A great disappointment to Doris and myself was all I could determine as we wheeled into the driveway.

Chapter 2

Yes, I did have orders to the USS Kreighton. I was to leave my present duty station in April. Well that wasn't too bad. There was still time to pull a few strings to get those orders canceled. This gave me a couple of months. No sweat. It would be a piece of cake.

Those with whom I talked during February didn't give me much encouragement. Well, March passed and I was no better off than I was in February. These last six weeks were of no help and time was getting short. One month remained before doomsday.

I talked to the Commander of my outfit many times during this period and this was of no apparent good. The last couple of times I had talked to him, I wasn't asking for his help, I was pleading for it. I didn't want to go back to sea.

The way the game is played, my rating (specialty and pay grade) was to go to sea for eighteen months. After that, thirty-six months of shore duty. My last eighteen months of sea duty was from December until April with three full years in between. I just didn't think I could go through another one of their eighteen-month tours of sea duty. They had me and they knew it. Their game is called Navy Baseball. Either you play ball with them, or they'll shove the bat down your throat. This all started on the 7th of February, and I had re-enlistment for four more years on the 5th. I was theirs for another four years. Had I received these orders before re-enlisting we would have played a little bit of the Chiefs' baseball. I would have told them to take their orders to the USS Kreighton and cram them.

Well, spilled milk.

I still had to get these orders canceled.

"What! Mary has to have an emergency operation and you want to take emergency leave?" If it isn't one thing, it's another. Emergency operation. Emergency leave. What I need is emergency cancellation of my transfer orders.

My division officer for this past year had just about been worthless to the Navy, to the shop, and to me. He was a CWO4 with thirty years in the service and had one of the worst cases of a "short-timers attitude" I had ever seen. He would come into the shop each morning, eat his corn flakes, read his newspaper, and leave. Nobody knew where that man went or what he did. I did know he left the complete operation of the division to me.

Jerry Truex, a First Class Aviation Electronics Technician, my relief, was the only one aboard this station who was qualified to take over my duties. He and I worked together these past few years and when Mr. "Hide and Seek" started his disappearing act, I tutored Jerry in the operation of the division.

I was to leave in two weeks and he wanted emergency leave while his wife was in the hospital and during her convalescence.

On the telephone the Chief said, "Stand by a minute, Jerry. I'll go see the Commander and find out what he has to say about it. Better yet, you come along. You'll be able to explain it in detail better than I." The office of our department commander was in the building next to ours. I yelled outside of my office toward the other workers in the shop, "Going to the Commander's office." This was to let someone else know to catch the phone and where we'd be if we were needed.

After Jerry related his story, the Commander picked up the telephone and talked to the base Commanding Officer. He explained the situation over the phone and told us to stand by for the Captain to call back. The Commander told Jerry he was sorry to hear Mary had problems and that these things worked out okay. His wife had undergone similar surgery. The phone rang. It was the CO, and he said to give Jerry his leave and that my orders were extended for another thirty days.

I thought, "Mary, I'm sorry to look at it this way, but you have just procured me thirty-day stay of execution. Well, reprieve. Thanks. I'll send flowers."

Mary's operation had come and gone without complication almost as the Commander had related. My situation now passed beyond acute for I was to leave next week.

Doris and I rented a house in Long Beach through a real estate agency. We personally inspected several places suggested by the Realtor and made our choice. Doris would stay in Oakland for a few days to oversee the packing and shipping of our household effects.

All my wheeler-dealer operations had failed.

I'll get even somehow . . . just you wait and see. This guy isn't finished yet.

Chapter 3

With a suitcase in each hand, I reported to Long Beach as ordered.

As I stood on the pier looking at the ship, I set my suitcases down. I raised my right arm and with a clinched fist I shouted, "Thanks, but no-thanks for the invitation, and I am going to get even if it takes forever."

Before embarking I scrutinized my new home. The superstructure towered in the air and was adorned with radar antennae that reminded me of my first duty aboard an aircraft carrier.

I climbed the afterbrow and reported aboard to the on duty. I set my two suitcases near the bulkhead just inside the hangar deck and told the Chief I'd be back later to pick them up.

I climbed ladders and walked through passageways until I found myself strolling about the flight deck.

There were many small, canvas, temporary sheds. Some protected the shipyard workers from the sun. Some were used to house supplies and some of the tent-like structures shielded the welders arc from others workers' eyes. It didn't take me long to see all that I wanted.

I went back down to the hangar deck.

The elevator doors were opened and assorted sizes of hose and cables ran from the edge of the dry-dock to the ship. It made me think of a patient in a hospital receiving multiple intravenous transfusions. The ship's gray paint was mottled with red lead primer giving it a resemblance of a clown. The ship was in dry-dock and after having been aboard less than an hour, I had seen everything from the keel to the radar masts. From my perspective at some of the viewpoints, the size of the carrier appeared exaggerated. Surely this could be neither a fighting vessel of the United States Navy nor my new home for an unknown period of time.

When I stepped aboard the USS Kreighton, I knew I was going to get even with someone, somewhere, somehow.

The plot of my revenge came to life within the first week as I was checking-in aboard the Kreighton. I took my dear, old, sweet time about checking-in, and as I checked-in to the necessary departments and divisions, it became more apparent that it was possible. It could be done. I know good and well it could be done. A person could come aboard this ship, play the role of a sailor for nearly a year and then walk off as if nothing had happened.

Rather than be a true stowaway, he would become part of the crew. Who, among a crew of nearly 3000, would really know or care? To establish the identity and keep his name from any official documents would be necessary. It would be difficult for a man to live such a long impersonation. Each move might spell disaster to himself and any other person or persons associated with the hoax.

As the idea developed, I anticipated the immediate hurdles to be overcome. As a Chief Petty Officer, I thought

I could cope with or slide around the remainder. When I
finished checking-in, I was sure that it was a good idea and
that it was, without doubt, possible.

That is, I had myself convinced.

I would need some assistants. There are two places
where I would need collaborators. The first place would be
my department office and the second would have to be the
ship's personnel office. The fewer persons involved, the less
the risk of exposure.

What if someone else found out? What would he say or
do? Could I trust him and how far? What if he hated my
guts? If the whole thing fell through, I could visualize the
story in the newspaper.

"COURT-MARTIAL FOR A STOWAWAY"

*Chief Petty Officer Jack B. Wilson was charged with vio-
lation of Title 18 of the U.S. Code, Section 2199, Article
0767 of Navy Regulations, and numerous articles of the
Uniform Code of Military Justice. This is in connection
with his smuggling a stowaway aboard a United States
Naval vessel.*

*Captain Wayne A. Westland, commanding officer of the
USS Kreighton (CVS 53), disclosed today CPO Wilson
had harbored a nineteen-year-old civilian aboard the
Kreighton for the past year. He stated Wilson had in-
duced the young man to come aboard for the hoax to the
U.S. Navy before the ship's departure last December to
the Western Pacific.*

*Conviction to Wilson can mean a loss of all rights and
benefits of a military man with eighteen years of service. Maximum penalty could also include a dishonorable discharge.*

The Commanding Officer of the 44,000-ton anti-subma-
rine aircraft carrier indicated that a court-martial for the
stowaway is being considered.

Fully realizing the consequences, I maintained an opti-mistic attitude and decided leap right in. Now that I had myself convinced, I must first recruit the assistance of the department office yeoman.

After having been aboard about a month, I eyed my tar-get. Right off I knew he was going to help.

He didn't.

How to convince him was my first hurdle. I just couldn't walk up to him and ask, "How would you like to have a court-martial?" He would probably say "No thanks" and go on about his business. Somehow I will have to let him in on the ground floor or blackmail him. I'm not above black-mail. If I were to stick my neck out this far, blackmail would only add one more charge. In the event my colleague got bogged down in the muck and mire of any disciplinary ac-tion, he could possibly use my blackmail in his defense.

One evening after chow, I settled down in the Chiefs' Mess to watch the movie for the evening. It started, but I wasn't as interested as I thought. I left the mess to wander about the ship. I headed for the department office. When I arrived only Airman Gray was present.

"Hi, Chief. What's happening?"

I walked over to the door of the Commander's office. I opened it and checked. Nobody home. We were alone.

I asked, "Gray, how long have you been in the Navy?"

"A little over a two years."

"How long have you been aboard the Kreighton?"

"Almost two years."

"How do you like it?"

"The Navy or the ship? Never mind Chief, I'll tell you in two words, and you can apply the answer where your ever-loving, little, old heart desires."

I knew right then he was mine. Now I had to put him in my pocket. How? Would it be voluntarily or otherwise?

"Say, Gray, do you think you could get me a blank liberty card?"

"Sure, Chief. Why do you want one? You know Chiefs don't need them."

"Never mind the details. Just get me one."

"What section?"

I answered, "Doesn't matter."

"Section one, okay?"

"Sure."

He walked over to a four-drawer file cabinet, opened the top drawer, and pulled out a stack of liberty cards consisting of four colors. He pulled one off the top and handed it to me stating that it was section one.

"Who keeps track of these things?" I asked.

"Well, nobody so to speak. That is, when a new man, 3rd class or below, checks into the department, I issue him one. His division lets me know what section to put him in. I type up the card, assign a number from the log, and then the department head signs it. From then on, it's up to the division to keep track of it."

"Thanks a lot," I said and put the card in my shirt pocket. I left knowing I had started with the plan. I also knew I'd be back to get something else.

I used the next day wandering around the ship except for some time I spent in the Chiefs' Mess listening to some of their problems and gripes. Of course the major topic was Yard. Yard this, Yard that. It was understandable because we were in the Long Beach Naval Shipyards for repairs. The ships' problems and discrepancies were brought to the attention of the shipyard workers by work requests, and it was the Chiefs' responsibility to see to the completion of the work to be accomplished in their assigned spaces. I knew neither what had to be nor what should be accomplished in the Aviation Electronic spaces. The Chief I relieved had taken care of the major repairs and modification requirements. Besides, most of the work now being done throughout the ship was finishing up minor jobs for we were to go on sea trails soon.

I decided to depart, leaving the Chiefs with their problems and the deafening shipyard noise.

The next morning after quarters for muster, I went back to the department office to speak with Gray. I asked him to step outside onto the catwalk just outside the office. As we spoke in private, I asked if he knew any of the personnelmen in the ships' personnel office.

He answered, "Sure, Chief. I know most everybody there. What do you want?"

"You don't think you could come up with a blank ID card do you?" This was the clincher. If I persuaded him to get this, I would have three hurdles crossed; namely, my man in the department office, a man in the personnel office, and an ID card. Of course the man in the personnel office wouldn't know yet that he was mine.

"I don't know about that, Chief. That isn't the easiest thing in the world to get."

"Well, maybe you could start off by getting me a check-in card. You know, the one a guy has to have signed by medical, dental, post office, et cetera?"

Disgustedly he replied, "Chief! I know what a check-in card is." He continued, "No problem there, and I'll see about the other."

"Thanks. See you later."

For the time being, that was all I could do on that end. I had the seed planted. Now I wanted to see if it would take root and bear fruit.

My biggest problem was still in the air. Who? Who would go along for the ride? What type of person would volunteer and say, "May I go to jail?" Someone who would go along with this must be some kind of a nut. Where is the orchard that bears such?

My stowaway would have to be somewhat naive, someone who would be game enough to give up a year of his life, yet wise enough to keep his mouth shut. I would have to take him under my wing to tutor him in the ways of the Navy. It would be a fast course of what is taught in boot camp and what is learned in the first few months in the Navy.

In the meanwhile, there are many more minor obstacles to be overcome. I must procure a Geneva Convention card, an immunization card, berthing facilities, and of course, uniforms. The only problem with uniforms is what rate should he be?

Getting the man would be the big bridge and would have to be crossed when approached. The road had to be paved up to that point and this was in the mill. Anytime up to that, the whole thing could be dropped and nothing would be lost. Everything could be dropped up to the point where he first came aboard in uniform. Once he stepped aboard, the damage was done. Intent. That's all they need to prove in a court-martial. Just intent!

Nevertheless, I would have to purchase his uniforms. If it fell through shortly afterward, I would only be out that amount. Let's see now. Uniforms costs plus I would have to pay his wages, or give him some spending money, an allowance, for nearly a year. That would cost me near a couple thousand. If things fell through after I purchased the uniforms, and no court-martial, I would, in a way, still be ahead. As long as I could keep my head off the chopping block, I'd be willing to foot the bill.

We were finished with the dry-dock part of repairs and were now tied up at a pier. We were constantly loading equipment and supplies aboard.

Almost a month passed since I asked Gray for the ID card. I was alone when he walked into the Avionics office and said he had something for me, I momentarily forgot what it could be. He beamed with pride as he handed me the blank ID card and the blank check-in card. He had accomplished his mission and appeared to be truly proud of it.

When I asked who in the personnel office assisted in the procurement of these items, he refused to tell. Just to see what type of an assistant I had, I fished in my private file for the previously procured liberty card. I used a paper clip to put the three cards together.

"Well, let's go see the Executive Officer and see if you will tell him."

"Chief that's dirty pool. Why do you want to get me into trouble? I don't understand this. I've never done anything to you. As a matter of fact I've done everything you've asked."

"You're right. You have helped, so I'll tell you the reason behind this. I have intentions of bringing a stowaway on the next WestPac cruise. What's more, you're going to help."

He grinned and laughingly questioned, "You can't be serious?"

I didn't smile when I came back with, "I'm serious. That is on both counts. I'm bringing him aboard for count number one for count number two you're going to help. There is a third count also. The young man in the personnel office who stole this ID card is going to help. Now go down to the personnel office and tell this lad that you two are in trouble. Bring him up here at 1600 this afternoon. Tell him no more, no less. You two are in trouble."

"He's going to get bent."

"Fine. See you at 1600. One more thing," I paused and grinned as I said, "Thanks."

He shook his head and slammed the door on his way out.

So far it was easy, almost too easy. The road hadn't even started to go uphill. Getting the stowaway was going to be the big one and now that I had gone this far, another problem came up. WHEN? WHO and now WHEN? We were to have our first sea trials in two weeks. Would it really be necessary to get him aboard before then?

Impossible.

When Airman Gray and Personnelman Third Class Whitteker arrived in my office that afternoon, I knew Whitteker imagined he had "had it." I assured him he wasn't in trouble as I explained how I was going to get the stowaway on board and run the whole show. I explained to him his position in my scheme and that I would really need very little from him. His job would be similar to Gray's in that the name of my man could not be put on any sort of official document. Making sure nothing from the department head concerning my man was to get out of the department office would be Gray's job. The same concerning the personnel office would be up to Whitteker. This could not be over-stressed. If anything showed up at either office, I was to be notified. Immediately! It had to be cut and dried right there. Nothing, absolutely nothing of an official nature, could bear the name of my stowaway.

Whitteker got in his two cents worth.

"I think the guy was right when he wrote 'The Navy was a master plan designed by genius' to be carried out by idiots.' It's nothing more than a game to some of you clowns. Is it any wonder that I want out of this canoe club? Chief, I don't like the idea of being screwed over the way you did. However, I'll go along with this mess. Why? I'll tell you. I think it is just stupid enough to work and further more, I don't care."

I'm sure Whitteker left my office somewhat relieved about being in trouble. Now, even Gray seemed to be a little interested. I was also starting to feel proud of my hoax. It's the feeling one gets when he is getting ready to put something over on someone. It's sometimes called the thrill of the hunt. It could be called a prelude to revenge or even an adrenaline high.

God help me for if I stumble, the Captain is going to be right there to walk all over me.

Chapter 4

As I read in the "Plan-of-the-Day," liberty expires on board at 0600 for all hands, I thought, "Oh, what a familiar statement." Anytime that liberty expires before 0730 it's unusual, and this time was no exception. The ship was to get underway at 0830.

I could have kicked myself around a block. We were getting underway and I still had no stowaway. I was hoping with all my might I would be able to get him aboard before our first short cruise.

Since this cruise was to be only three days it would be perfect. He could find out what it is like to be aboard a ship and what the Navy really has to offer. If he changed his mind I would have plenty of time to find another man. Also, I wouldn't need all the documents I had procured, and they wouldn't be wasted. Another important feature of this short cruise was I might possibly borrow some uniforms from one of the guys in my division.

The 1MC general announcing system blurted, "The Officer-of-the-Deck is shifting his watch from the quarterdeck to the bridge." I checked my watch . . . 0745. These guys are serious. They do have intentions of getting this big monster out to sea.

"The ship is underway. The ship is underway," was the next thing I heard passed over the 1MC. Again I checked the time . . . 0853. The ability to get underway within three minutes of the scheduled time was really amazing. I truly expected more near an hour and a half.

Underway. After three years I was again part of the sea-going Navy. Deep inside of me there was a feeling, a strange feeling, a nostalgic feeling that this indeed is where a sailor belongs. It's a sense of belonging to one of the greatest fighting forces ever assembled. No way, they weren't going to get to me by that method. I enjoy quite a sense of patriotism, but now I've no choice but to discard that feeling every time it comes up. I was determined to maintain the feeling I had a few months ago about going aboard a ship, going to sea, and toward the Navy! I finished eating my evening meal and decided on a sightseeing tour of the flight deck. The sun had just touched the horizon as I reached the last step up the catwalk onto the flight deck.

Water. Water. Water. Everywhere, water. What else could be expected? We were a lonely vessel upon a vast ocean, no escort destroyers or any other type of ship, no land in sight, nothing but a 900-foot ship upon a 2000-mile ocean. Wait a minute. There was something else out here, weather! I thought the ship had a little too much movement. Or did it? I can't remember. The last ship I was on was a hundred and fifty feet longer than this one and also somewhat wider. Was this movement normal for this size of ship? I didn't believe so.

I walked across the flight deck, wandered about on one of the catwalks, and again gazed at my environment. The weather was without doubt with us. The wind had picked up and the ground swells were causing the ship to pitch more than I thought to be usual.

As I walked across the flight deck and looked forward toward the bow, I could see how much the ship was really pitching. I jumped down into the catwalk and measured the flight deck against what could still be seen of the horizon.

Not only was the ship pitching more than I thought, it was rolling more than I had realized.

I can't even recall the last time I gave any concern to the movement of a ship. After a short time on board a person begins to accept it a part of life and ignores it unless it is quite bad, such as in a storm.

Only twelve hours out of Long Beach and the ocean is this rough? I don't believe it, yet I'm starting to get a headache. I think I'll go below to the Chiefs' Quarters, take a couple aspirin and relax. The paperwork today has tired me, and now, the ship's movement. My stomach doesn't seem to be quite right either, so I know I'll go below back to the Chiefs' Quarters.

I started back across the flight deck to the starboard catwalk. Just after I had taken a few steps I ran into another Chief. "Hi." Then I noticed. "Are you all right? You look a little woozy."

"It's this rocking and rolling. It's getting to me."

I replied, "I thought it was me until I looked out across the horizon."

"It's this ship. It amplifies every ripple in the water. The thing is lopsided, distorted, or something. I don't know what it is, but it pitches and rolls as no other aircraft carrier can. Right now the only thing that seems to help me is the fresh air in my face. Excuse me, I . . . ." He relieved his stomach of its burden and then turned to me. "Sometimes the fresh air doesn't seem to help all that much."

I know anyone can get seasick so I said, "Yeah, I know what you mean."

I thought it was me. I was glad there were others who were looking pale. Not that I wanted anyone to get sick, I just wanted to reassure myself I wasn't the only one. Maybe it's a good thing that I didn't get my stowaway on board today. He would have surely chickened out after the first day. I don't think he'd even want to finish this three-day cruise. Yet, on the other hand, if he could make it through this, the rest would be easy.

Here I was worrying about what he would think and how he would feel. I didn't even know who he was going to be. That's what I should've been thinking about.

"Take two aspirin and call me tomorrow" is the standard sickbay treatment, so rather than bother them, I diagnosed my own case, took my own prescription, and slept.

The morning brought a beautiful day and a calm ocean. It was the calm I was wanting. My thoughts were still with the previous evening, and again I was thinking about my stowaway.

Not everything was so rosy. My stomach was cramping, so I decided to go to sickbay. I had noticed this feeling in my stomach became more frequent in these past few months. I waited until after the 0800 sick call, and when I was able to see a doctor, it was near 1000. He poked and probed a bit and asked a bunch of seemingly irrelevant questions. I knew he was going to give me some Dramamine for motion sickness so what was it with the other dumb stuff?

"I've read your record and with the answers you've given me I suspect you have ulcers. What stage, I don't know, but I am positive that is your problem.

"From what I gather, you're not eating enough, you're eating the wrong type of food, you're not getting proper rest, you're too worried about something, and to be quite candid, you're in terrible shape.

"First, no aspirin, next no Alka Seltzer, no cokes, no beer, and definitely, no whiskey."

"You've just slit my throat, Doc."

"Maybe worse yet, I've just got started. I've got some stuff here that you'll swear is pure chalk and water. Read the directions. Start carrying some antacid tablet of your choice. Take the liquid as primary relief and when it isn't available, use the tablets. If you can't straighten out your diet, I can. Believe me, you don't want that to happen. Start getting into good rest habits."

"You've just ruined my social life," I interrupted.

"Now about the worrying side. From what I know about you, you are in no financial troubles and no marital problems. You've recently reported aboard and are evidently upset over that. Accept the fact that you are going to be on board for some time and stop worrying about it.

"Take this prescription to the pharmacy, have it filled, follow the directions, get to feeling better, and come back for a social call. You see I know your wife. I met her at a golf tournament a few years back. She and my wife are competitors, yet good friends. Has Doris ever mentioned Frances Swanson?"

"Certainly." I smiled and stated, "You're Doc Swanson. Doctor Matt Swanson?"

"Yes. And now you are smiling. Stop worrying and take the medicine. See you later."

"Right. Thanks Doc. Maybe some day we will get a chance to have a social chat." I smiled as I teased, "We could shoot the bull over a few beers."

He looked at me with a scowl, shook his head indicating no, and said, "Right!"

Well, I took some of the medicine and some of his advice. The medicine was, as he said, pure chalk. I swore off alcohol, . . . while aboard ship, and I did consider better resting habits. Most of the time I would think of who, who could I get to be my stowaway.

Constant thoughts of "who" finally paid off.

Yes, there was a person! Why hadn't I thought of him before? Again I said to forget with the world of reality. I had finally thought of the person. He would be a perfect fit, tailor made. What more could I ask? I was happy. I was wildly smiling to myself. If someone had taken a close look at me as I was walking up to my office, seeing someone as happy as I am, they'd have surely thought that I had only one oar in the water.

After I reached my office on the O 2 level, I called the AIMD office to speak with Gray.

"Gray, Chief Wilson here. I've a job for you. Just as soon as you can get a break, come up to the Avionics Office."

"I'm not doing anything right now. I'll be right up."

The compartment in which the Avionics Division Office is located is in fact a portion of the Avionics Calibration lab. That is where they calibrate and recalibrate the electronic test equipment.

When Gray arrived, I asked the technician to step outside while Gray and I had a private conversation. Thank goodness the division officer wasn't present. His desk is directly behind mine, and I could hardly have asked the Lieutenant to leave.

I told Gray I had a prospect for a stowaway and told him of my immediate plans. I also told him I might need more documents.

"Chief, you know Whitteker and I talked about your loony idea. You realize he has an attitude about the Navy.

He uses the old expression that all he wants out of the Navy is himself, and as for me, I wanted to go to AT "A" School, but that looks pretty dim. As long as I'm stuck in the Department Office, I don't think there's any chance. So that leaves me with a 'Why not?' attitude. I'm not going anywhere, anyhow."

He reassured me that between Whitteker and himself, they would procure all that would be necessary. At least all that they could think of that such a person would need.

He left enthused with his assignment and I was enthused with my choice for a stowaway.

A heart murmur or something like that was what Jimmy had. Dolly told me this about five years ago when Doris and I had lived across the street from them in San Diego.

Paul, Jimmy's father, had completed a hitch in the Air Force about fifteen years ago and felt as though it had a little educational value. Nothing more. However he wasn't shy about finishing his college under the GI Bill of Rights. He had been quite insistent about Jimmy's going to college. I wonder what he would say if Jimmy skipped a year between high school and college.

Wonder I did for the next two days. As I pondered over all aspects, everything seemed to fit perfectly. James L. Martin, high school graduate, "A" minus student, not physically fit for Uncle Sam, you are going to become a pseudo sailor.

Chapter 5

The first Saturday morning after we returned to port, Doris and I had our bags packed and headed for a weekend vacation in San Diego. Vacation? I was going on business. Doris had called Dolly to make sure they would be home for the weekend and to find out if they would mind our coming down. Dolly was pleased we were coming and said Paul was already lighting up the grill.

A friendly reception and a revival of old friendships occupied the first hour. A cold beer and a sizzling steak along with stories of passed experiences occupied the second.

Forget this idle talk. I wanted to get down to business. Anxiety was making it impossible for me to maintain my enthusiasm. The women, leaving Paul and I alone on the patio, went into the house discussing who lived in our old house and other general gossip.

"Well Chiefie, how's the Navy treating you?"

I was glad he opened the conversation about the service.

"Not bad, not bad at all, Paul." I paused and then said, "No Paul, that's not true. As a matter of fact, that's the reason I came down this weekend." I wanted to get to the point as soon as possible.

"Don't cry to me about the service. I did my four and got out. You lifers are all the same, stick it out for sixteen to eighteen years and have nothing. Then see a guy like me who put in his four, took the GI Bill for college, now an engineer for an aircraft company, making twice, maybe three times your money and not having to move around like a nomad."

When he paused, I jumped in, "Wait a minute! Hold on. I'm not complaining about that and besides I heard the same story from you a hundred times when I lived across the street. You do make twice the money that I do, but you have twice the expenses. As far as money goes, Doris makes more than you and I put together. I want to tell you exactly why I came down."

Leaving Jimmy out, I told him my story of the past year and my idea of the stowaway. He commented, "You're insane. That's ridiculous. What makes you think you could possibly get away with such?"

"I've already told you that. It's such a lax situation, and nothing is ever double-checked. I could put you on there in a Chiefs uniform and nobody would ever question you as to who you are or why you are on board. If it should accidentally come up, you could feed them a line of bull. It's never checked out. Mostly because nobody cares or pays attention."

He came back with, "I've seen similar in the Air Force. I know it isn't checked, but why would anybody in his right mind want to go along with your stupid scheme? What's in it for them?"

"Well," I said, "one thing is just knowing that you've pulled one over on the big boys. Another would be the travel aspect, free passage to the Orient and all that garbage. Of course, there's always the adventure story. You know, one step ahead of the law, your heart beats faster and, well, you've heard all that malarkey in detective stories and TV shows. At the end, the glory of accomplishment."

"That still doesn't really explain it," he said.

"Evidently I'm not getting through to you."

"Evidently."

"Let me try again. Let's say that someone didn't especially care for the service. That he's always heard how rotten an outfit it is and he'd become cynical by these biased opinions. Or let's take a guy who would like to go to Japan or Hong Kong and knows the probability of his ever going is small. You know, no money, has to constantly work for a living, and such. Let me ask you this. Do you think you could pack your bags and head for Japan tomorrow? No you couldn't! You make at least twice the money I do but still you're tied down. Right?"

"Okay. I concede two points. I am tied to my job and my savings couldn't stand a trip to the Orient," he replied. "But I still wouldn't be interested."

"Now, the next point. Let's assume you did have the desire to go, the desire to travel if you please, and didn't want to obligate yourself to the service to accomplish such. Now would you be interested in going? It would be like taking the gravy wouldn't it?"

"You might say that," he answered, "but I still think you're insane. It's just plain stupid!"

"Now, let's go one step farther. Keeping you in the picture, let's assume you have the desire to travel, adventure, or what have you, and you wouldn't mind joining the service, but you're physically disabled. Now, to become my stowaway is not necessarily a hoax, but rather an opportunity. Isn't it?"

"Yeah, but I'm still not going with you," he said jokingly.

"I don't want you, Paul. I want Jimmy to be that stow-away."

I would have to say that just as he was taking a drink of beer. He spewed it out of his mouth, choked, gagged, and some even ran out of his nose.

"Dolly!" he yelled, just as soon as he was able. He followed it with, "Dolly, come out here!"

She and Doris came running out to the patio. Surely they must have thought I had shot Paul.

"What's happened?" Dolly questioned excitedly.

"This idiot wants Jimmy to stowaway on his boat for a year."

"Ship, Paul. Ship." Thoughts of correcting him flashed in my mind, but I concluded this was neither the time nor place.

Dolly looked at me and laughingly stated, "You can't be serious."

"I am serious. Would you like for me to explain it to you or would you rather harbor Paul's biased opinion?"

Dolly said, "Please explain. This has to be interesting."

I should have been insulted by their remarks, but I was too serious about it to let them get to me. Besides, I needed Jimmy.

Doris was standing in the doorway with a hurt look on her face, and her stance implied the same. She was aware of the whole project, as it had developed. The more I explained it to her, the more she allowed me to convince her that it would work. Doris had become as excited over it as I and now with Dolly and Paul's remarks, she too, seemed hurt.

Again I related the story of the past year. Paul kept interrupting with snide remarks, but Dolly listened with interest. When I finished, she had an expression that would make you think of a big question mark. She turned to Paul showing him the same enthralled expression and with somewhat of a curious gleam in her eyes.

Paul looked at her and said, "No Dolly. No! The guy is sick. He's crazy. Like I told him, it's just plain stupid."

She came back at him. "Why wouldn't it work? It seems to me he's gone through a lot of trouble to work out each detail such as the assistants, the credential, clothes, berthing, and all. Why not?"

"Come on, Dolly, get serious. You're both sick. They lock people up for less than that." He looked at Doris and asked, "Doris? You too?"

Doris nodded her head yes and a satisfied, sneaky grin grew on her lips as a reply to Paul's query.

"No! No way. Jimmy is going to college," Paul stated bluntly.

I replied, "I didn't say he wasn't."

"Why does he have to start this fall?" Dolly asked.

"Wait a minute. Wait just a minute," he said to Dolly as he stood and walked around. "This nut shows up with a hair brained scheme, the rest of you flip, and now you're trying to make me out to be a villain. No thanks. NO THANKS!"

Trying to follow Paul around with my eyes, I got back into the conversation saying, "Paul, will you cool it a minute? Would you do me the favor of asking Jimmy?"

"No, no way! I'm not asking anyone anything. I'm telling you N. O., no! And that goes for you too, Dolly. You're all crazy. Why not plan something simple like a bank robbery? Brinks, perhaps? It would probably work again. Take on a few thousand cops and the FBI, but not the whole United States Government. Come on! Get serious!"

"Quit being so melodramatic. Sit down!" Dolly said, seeming to be laying down the law, and Paul obeyed. "I

think it should be up to Jimmy. Besides, it will only postpone his college."

"Yeah, postpone it. Would you believe five to ten years?
That plus some stupid fine that the government always
wants to throw in. You know, like, $10,000."

I rebutted, "That is provided we get caught. Paul, listen to me. I'm betting a minimum of eighteen years of my
life and a dishonorable discharge that we can go through
with it. Don't you think I know what this means? If I
thought for one minute it wouldn't work, I wouldn't be
betting my life that it would. I'm betting my past and my
future. Sure, Jimmy would be betting high also, and I think
it should be his decision."

"I am not going to let it be his decision," he stated
emphatically. "But I will tell him of your proposed fiasco.
Just as soon as he gets back this evening, I'll tell him."
Paul stood up, paused, and then turned to me. "One more
thing, Jack. I'm not going to give you any more beer for
the rest of the weekend. It makes you dingy. Boy, do you
get carried away."

Paul was shaking his head as he walked into the
house, went to the refrigerator. He got out another beer
and opened it for himself. Evidently he was starting to
get serious. He never offered me another one. He walked
into the living room, turned on the television, and
flopped on the couch.

As I watched him through the patio doors, Dolly must
have sensed what I was thinking. "Care for another beer,
Jack?"

"Thanks, Dolly. You're sweet."

When Dolly handed me the beer, she interrupted my
thoughts of how I was going to explain my stowaway
idea to Jimmy. He was the one who had to be sold on the
entire project.

"Dolly, I want you to know Paul could be right about this thing. It is serious. However, he does get carried away with his exaggerations. Maybe I should just mention it to Jimmy and let it rest for a while."

"Listen, Jack. I could tell from the text of your story you've planned and worked hard on the details of this thing. Also, that you're deeply excited over it. Last, but not least, I know you'd be taking a big risk. If you can sell it to Jimmy, he and I will sell it to Paul."

"Dolly, I know it will work."

"We'll discuss it further when Jimmy comes home. Paul is thinking about it now. I can tell by the way he stares at the ceiling. He isn't paying a bit of attention to the television. It's always the same when he has a serious decision."

Again she and Doris went back into the house. This time they left me alone on the patio.

"Are my thoughts twisted now?" I thought. "How am I going to put this into the proper sequence so I can sell it to Jimmy? I want to get him alone as I explain it so the great actor won't interrupt me. Maybe I should explain it with Paul sitting in so I will have another chance to sell it to him. I just don't know. I think I'm more confused over this thing than I've ever been."

I stared at the bottle of beer in my hand, knowing I shouldn't be drinking it. I could feel that my stomach wasn't feeling right, but at this moment I just didn't care.

I kept thinking of the scheme and at this point concluded, I don't know. I just don't know.

I must have been thinking out loud because Doris walked out onto the patio, lovingly massaged my shoulders, and asked me what I wanted. She said she heard me say something as she walked near the patio door. I assured her nothing was wrong and said that I must have been thinking aloud.

As I began to relax under her gentle massage, we heard a car drive into the driveway.

It had to have been Jimmy for as I turned to look into the house, I saw Doris looking toward Paul.

Chapter 6

Jimmy announced his arrival in the house with, "Hi, Dad. Whose car is . . . ? Hello, Mrs. Wilson. Hi, Jack." His eyes were searching as he walked in, and it didn't take him long to spot us at the patio doors. He came over to us, gave Doris a quick hug, and shook my hand.

"I should have known it was you. You're driving a brand new Buick. Come on, Jack, there are other cars you know. It's good to see you. How you been?"

I answered, "Good Jimmy. And you? We always get a great buy on Buick's. Remember? Doris' father is my friendly dealer."

"I'm great, but knock off the Jimmy stuff. That went out a couple years ago. Everyone calls me Jim except Mom and Dad. Hi, Mom."

"Well, it is nice to know I'm not completely ignored." His mother followed that with, "Hungry?"

"Sort of . . ." He turned back to Doris and me. "What brings you down here? Heard you're living in Long Beach. That right?"

I got in a, "Yeah" before Paul sat upright on the couch.

"Jimmy. Come in here a minute," Paul interrupted with a demanding tone.

"Okay, Dad. Excuse me, Mrs. Wilson, Jack."

I knew what Paul was going to do. He was going to ruin my whole project right now. I wanted to say, "Let me tell him," but decided against it. Butterflies were carrying my stomach to the stars. I was scared. As I turned to look at Doris, I could see she had been studying my expression. She could see my concern for I knew it was written all over my face. We turned back to Paul.

"Jimmy, Jack drove down this weekend to talk to you. He has something very important to say to you. Now listen Son, I want you to pay close attention and weigh what he says for it may affect the rest of your life. Do you understand?"

"Sure, Dad."

"Pay attention. And don't give me any of that "Sure, Dad" stuff. I'm serious, and Jack is very serious. It's that important. Now do you understand?"

Jimmy's expression changed from a friendly boy to a serious young man. He looked at me, then back to his dad. Paul knew he had received his answer.

I thought, "Well thank you very much, Paul. You surprised me. I'm glad, because if anything goes sour now it will be my fault."

"Dolly, come in here. We're going to go over this thing again. Slow and easy with all the details that Jack can think of. Doris, you too, come on in. Turn off the TV, Son."

We gathered in the living room. Everyone looked at each other, and then everyone focused their attention and was looking directly at me. I knew I had center stage from here on.

This was my moment of truth. My hands were sweating. I took a deep breath and tried to relax. The butterflies were still there. I took in another deep breath and let it out slowly before I spoke.

"Jim, the first of June I was transferred to the USS Kreighton, an aircraft carrier out of Long Beach. In my first week on board, I became aware of how relaxed the ship is about who comes and goes aboard. I also noticed how easy it would be for a complete stranger to come on board and stay for a while. You know, a stowaway. However, in order to stay aboard for any length of time and go completely unnoticed a stowaway would have to be in uniform. Added to this were thoughts of, 'Why couldn't a person do it and get away with it? What would cause a person in such a capacity to get caught?' I answered my own questions by playing a mental game of chess. For each move, there was a counter move, a defense. I asked myself many questions, some quite far out. For each question I searched for, and found, an answer. After two or three months, I had all the details worked out. A person could live aboard that ship for two weeks and never be noticed. If he stayed on board longer than that, he would have to become part of the crew, and the risks would increase with each passing day. He would become familiar with the crew and then there would be questions. Personal questions.

"To avoid being obvious, the stowaway would have to check-in as a new man reporting for duty. To make the plan foolproof, the stowaway would need a sponsor who would help him. In the event the stowaway ever got into trouble, it would be the responsibility of the sponsor to get him out of the jam smooth enough where there would be no questions asked about it later. It just couldn't be a one-man job for such an extended period of time.

"There would be no personnel record for this man, so he couldn't become involved with the personnel department. There would be no medical record so he couldn't become involved with those people and it would be the same with disbursing. No monies paid, none mentioned.

"Also at the end of his stowaway period, there could be no record of his ever being aboard. If there were records, he could be charged with a federal crime and the documents would convict him. The penalty would be ten years in a federal penitentiary, a $10,000 fine, or both. I researched what laws would be broken and have approximated the penalty. Multiple indictments and convictions could compound the sentence.

"Along with this, he would be carrying the label of a convicted felon for the rest of his life. This in itself would be very damaging to a person's social status along with many unmentionable mental stresses.

"I am positive I could take such a stowaway on board and get away clean. If I got caught doing this, I too could be convicted and my sentence would be five to ten years, a dishonorable discharge, and the loss of all rights and benefits. Eighteen years of service shot. Doris would be a prison widow for five to ten years, and then married to a guy who was dishonorably discharged.

"This would be very damaging to her professional career also.

"Well, that's the background. There are more details. Assuming I did take a stowaway aboard, I would have to make sure he would play it exactly as I dictated. It would have to be what you could call blind obedience.

"There would be expenses for uniforms, toilet articles, and of course, spending money. If I were to take on such an obligation, I would pay for all these necessities out of my pocket.

"However, I've thought it over and have discussed it with Doris. She has agreed that if I am sure, that if I want to put my whole life down as the ante, she will put hers right along side of it. I have in fact decided to do so. I've decided to stow away a man on that ship from about six months to a year.

"I already have the necessary documents to establish the man as a sailor. I also have two collaborators on board who are willing to bet all they have that it can be done. It would have to be teamwork. As of right now, there are two things lacking."

I paused, looked around, looked back straight at Jimmy and said, "That is you and your uniforms."

You could have heard a pin drop.

Jimmy was now the center of attraction. No one spoke. All our eyes turned to him. He turned to his dad as if to question him. Still no one spoke. Then he turned to his mother. He acted as if he wanted to question her. Neither Paul nor Dolly said a word. By his actions, I assumed Jimmy was thinking not only of what I had said, but also what Paul had said to him as we sat down.

Jimmy looked at the floor for a few seconds, got up, walked to the front door, paused, and went out. He never said a word. We heard the motor of his car start and we heard the sounds of the car driving away.

Everyone looked around at each other. Paul slapped his hands on his knees and broke what seemed to be an eternal silence with, "Anyone care for a beer? Perhaps a shot of bourbon?" He looked at me and shaking his head said, "You gotta be sick!"

I smiled as I said, "Yes Paul, I think I could go for the latter, and if you don't mind, I'll impose upon your generosity and take a double."

He looked toward Doris.

She responded, "Thanks, Paul. I could go for a shot also but for Jack, please, not a double."

Paul looked at Dolly, and she answered his eyeing question with, "Break out the bottle. I'll get the glasses. It looks as though it may be a long night."

Three, maybe four, hours passed. I hardly noticed the darkness creeping in until Dolly rose and walked toward the light switch. Conversation, since Jimmy departed, consisted of short questions answered with shorter replies.

Dolly stood up and turned on the lights, as she said, "No need for us to sit in the dark." She paused, and then spoke again, "How about a sandwich?"

She hardly had the words out of her mouth when once again we heard the sound of Jimmy's car driving up.

As he walked in the house, Paul and I looked at him—neither of us spoke. Again the place was as silent as a morgue for a short while.

This silence was broken as Dolly nonchalantly commenced to prepare the sandwiches, and Doris rattled silverware as she began to set the table.

Dolly spoke of what was available and asked for preferences for sandwiches. She and Doris prepared and served them.

I took one bite of my sandwich, chewed for a minute and then spoke. Someone had to speak and since no one else would, I said very simply, "Jim?"

Jim had sat down at the table and took a bite of the sandwich that his mother placed in front to him. After he swallowed he asked, "Is the decision mine? If not, Dad, what do you have to say about it?" Jim continued to eat his sandwich. His composure was more relaxed than mine.

Paul said nothing.

"Mom, what do you have to say?"

She, as Paul, said nothing.

"If the decision is entirely mine and with the stakes that Jack is wagering on the fact that we can do it, then we'll do it. However, I do want to hear the whole thing again with a few more of the details thrown in."

Chapter 7

Tuesday after Labor Day was another workday for me. I went to the ship thinking about Jimmy.

Before Doris and I left San Diego, Jimmy and I went over the operation three or four times, and he seemed to thoroughly understand the complete concept. He said he could wrap up his affairs by the first of September and would be in Long Beach soon after Labor Day.

Just before the lunch hour, I received a call to report to the gangway. I had a visitor. I reported as requested and discovered my guest to be Doris.

"What are you doing here? I've asked you many times not to come where I'm working."

"I know," she replied, "but I thought you would like to know as soon as possible that Jimmy is here."

"Here?"

"He's sitting out in the car. Can you get off to go out and talk with him?"

I replied, "Wait here for a few minutes. I'll be right back."

I went down to the Chiefs' Mess and located the AIMD Leading Chief. I told him I had an out-of-town guest and was going to take the rest of the day off. He assured me that it would be all right and would let only those he deemed necessary know where I had gone.

As I went back up to the gangway, I could see by Doris' pacing that her patience was growing thin with my absence. I told her I had taken the rest of the day off.

We departed the ship, and she escorted me to the car where Jimmy was waiting.

"Hi, Jack."

"Hi, Jim. I see you are still interested in giving this thing a whirl. Do you remember correcting me on the Jim vs. Jimmy stuff? Well, forget the Jack stuff. From now on it is Chief or Chief Wilson. Okay?"

"Yes, sir. On both accounts"

"There is another one. It's not sir either. Remember, Chief or Chief Wilson, never 'sir.'"

"Do you want to stowaway for a short cruise and see what you think or do you want to leap in with both feet?"

"Well, sir."

I interrupted. "Chief."

"Well, Chief, if you're still as positive as you were, I figure we may as well shoot the works."

"Meaning?"

"Go for broke on the first shot."

"Did you have to use the expression 'go for broke'?" Doris was behind the wheel so I said, "Drive us over to the Exchange and buy this sailor some uniforms. The Clothing and Small Stores isn't open now or we would buy some of his things there. Know your sizes?"

"Close."

"Good. You won't be able to go into the Exchange because of the checking of ID cards. Doris and I will go in and buy some of the things that you will need immediately. Start giving us some sizes. Is there anything you need in the way of toilet articles?"

He began to rattle off his sizes. Doris nodded her head as he done so.

We purchased a few of the uniforms Jim would need. While there we purchased a Blue Jackets Manual, an overnight bag, a bag for his toilet articles, and the articles he mentioned. Doris purchased some things she needed for herself, and we went back to the car.

"Had anything to eat?"

"No, sir. Ah, Chief."

"Good. I didn't get a chance to eat aboard ship. Let's go to the cafeteria and get a bite to eat. We can kill some time, and then go to the base Clothing and Small store for the rest of your uniforms. They're cheaper there. I bought these things here because I don't want to purchase everything in one place at one time, and I didn't want everything to look exactly alike or brand new. We'll take care of the small stuff later."

After eating, we drove to the Small Store. There we bought undershirts, shoes, socks, white hats, and more uniforms. This would be all that he would need or could use for the time being.

We paid a visit to the Barber Shop. We had quite a laugh over his haircut. He went from a longhaired hippie to practically a skinhead in the matter of minutes.

When we arrived at the house, Doris set up the sewing machine and commenced to tailor the uniforms. She also sewed on the required rating badges as I instructed.

I set up the ironing board and did what I could.

Jim tried on each uniform and commented of its strange feeling. "I've seen sailors in San Diego all my life, but never had any idea of how their uniforms felt or what they went through to get one on. These jumpers are something else."

"Jim, I want you to wear the dungarees around the house as much as possible. I also want you to put on the whites at least once a day.

"Wear them for a while, take them off, fold them up, and put them away. I'll show you how to fold your uniforms as they teach you in boot camp.

"I'm going to get you a bucket. I want you to wash your dungarees in the bucket and I want you to learn how to iron them. This is so you'll know a bit more of boot camp and be able to comment on how to wash clothes in a bucket. The reason for this is for you to become familiar with the uniforms. Familiar with the way they are worn, the way they are washed, ironed, and folded.

"Any comments?"

"I really didn't give much thought to this aspect."

He took the next uniform Doris finished and went to his assigned bedroom to try it on. When he returned, I said, "Here is one of the presents I bought you at the exchange. Now for your first lesson in spit shining shoes." I demonstrated a short time and handed him the can of shoe polish, the water, and some cotton balls. I said, "This is your present." I'm sure he was just tickled pink, as he showed me quite a scowl.

I walked over to where Doris was sitting. I put my arm around her and said, "Well Honey, we've started. I'm still positive we can do it with no problem. I've made arrangement with Whitteker to get Jim's ID picture and card laminated. Next is to get him a check-in card.

"We won't have to get the liberty card and the Geneva Convention card. These will be automatic after he checks in. There are a few more preparatory items I have to take care of on the ship and then I'll be ready. The rest will have to be up to Jim. Ah, Martin."

She replied, "Yes, we've started, and I've my work cut out. Why don't you sit down for a while? Relax. Your nervousness is getting to me. I'm sure it's getting to Jim. You're acting as I would suspect an expectant father to act."

Chapter 8

During the first week Jim read the "Blue Jackets Manual," and we discussed what he read. During this time we established him as a reserve on a two-year active duty assignment and set his enlistment to expire shortly after the time the ship would be returning from the WestPac cruise. This also meant he would be reporting to the Kreighton from another duty station. One where he spent the past year.

With this set up he would had to have graduated from high school a year earlier than he actually did, so we set his graduation date and his birth date accordingly.

We determined some time ago that his rate would be an AZAN, which is an Aviation Maintenance Administrationman. (This is the rating badge that Doris had sewn on his uniforms.) This job would entail administrative work, and I needed an AZ to work for me in my office.

Yes, James L. Martin, you are going to have to be a historian of fictional events, dates, and above all, a master liar.

Sometimes during the quizzing of his name, rate, service number, and other fabrications, he would make a mistake so we would start again from the beginning.

Later I asked, "What was your last duty station? What was the name of your last division officer?" This is where we would stop for we hadn't considered this angle.

Jim asked, "Who? Who was my last division officer?"

"I don't know. Pick an uncle on your mother's side and make a lieutenant out of him. You can't look to me for an answer to something like that after we get aboard ship. You're going to have to do your own ad lib lying."

Munching on popcorn and drinking Cokes, we continued with the quizzing. "What's the date you commenced active duty? What's your service number?"

This went on and on. He continued to read, and Doris and I would once again quiz him. She was real good with the questions. She would question him on items such as his pay and advancements. These must be the things that are important to women.

There was no television during this learning period. Several times I thought the kid was getting the "third degree." It was as if the police was questioning him over some crime in which he was the prime suspect.

Thank goodness this guy had an excellent memory.

Sometimes we asked him questions we didn't know the answers to, and he would give us a reply without hesitation.

"How big is the USS Enterprise?"

"It is 1102 feet long, 252 feet wide and has a displacement of 80,000 tons."

"Are you sure?"

"No, but I'm close. Give me a little slack."

We laughed together.

That was the type of answer I was looking for because no one carries this information around in his head unless he is or has been stationed aboard the Enterprise.

I was well pleased with the first week.

Saturday after breakfast I said, "Martin, Whitteker has the duty today. He's the Third Class Personnelman I've told you about. Well, I've made arrangements with him to process your ID card this morning. That means we will go aboard the Kreighton and have your picture taken and the card laminated. He already has all the information typed on it and has it signed. Forgery, that's another charge we can throw in. It lacks your signature and picture.

"When we go aboard, do nothing, absolutely nothing, but observe everything I do when arriving and departing the ship. Pay particular attention to the salutes and asking permission to come aboard and permission to depart.

Once you are in uniform you will have to be doing the same thing. The only difference is that when you go aboard and leave, as a sailor, you will have to show the Chief of the Watch your ID and liberty card. Today, again I repeat, do nothing. Act dumb and observe."

I gave Doris a peck of a kiss and said; "See ya in an hour or so. Ready, Martin?"

"Sure, Chief."

I said, "If your heart is pounding instead of beating, let's go."

We went aboard with no problems. I signed Martin in the guest logbook as James Claiborne, and we proceeded down ladders and through passageways to the Personnel Office.

After the introduction, Whitteker took Martin's picture with an instant ID camera. He already had the name board set up with Martin's name and service number so the card was ready to be laminated within minutes.

Martin and Whitteker seemed to have hit it off quite well and since only the three of us were there, Whitteker gave Martin a tour of the office and an explanation of the personnel business. Whitteker used my service record as a demonstrator while explaining what the personnel business was all about. Throughout the tour, Martin asked surprisingly intelligent questions.

While they were talking Martin said to Whitteker, "The Chief said he got my service number from you. How did you come up with it?"

"I got it from a deceased file."

"How morbid," replied Martin. He turned and looked at me, "You mean I'm running around with some dead man's service number?"

I shrugged my shoulders and responded, "It won't be duplicated."

When the buzzer on the lamination timer sounded, Whitteker removed the ID card and trimmed it on the paper cutter. When he finished, he gave it to Martin and said, "Welcome aboard, sailor. How do you feel?"

Martin looked at the picture on the card, looked at Whitteker, and replied, "Scared."

Again Whitteker said, as a double agreement, "Welcome aboard."

I mumbled an "Amen" to myself. We left Whitteker smiling and shaking his head.

After we departed the ship, I said, "Well, Sailor, let's go buy you some more uniforms so you can have some more stenciling, washing, and ironing to do."

In reply, I received a disgusted, "Thanks a lot."

From the ship we went to the Small Stores and purchased more uniforms. From there we drove around the base for a while. I pointed out the officer passers-by and told him of their rank.

Jim and I had relieved a bit of the tension while driving around the base and when we reached home we found out where all the tension had been stored. Doris was furious. She clouded up and rained on both of us.

"Where have you been? I thought you were already in trouble. You didn't have any consideration for my part of this." She was so furious that after she let off her steam she started to sob a little and said, "I've been a nervous wreck since you've been gone."

She was right. We were gone for about three hours and as for myself, I never gave a thought of her waiting for us to return.

Chapter 9

Sunday meant back to the grindstone for Martin. He stenciled his name and service number on his new uniforms and commenced the laundering of the ones he wore that week. I instructed that the dungarees were to be scrubbed by hand and were to look at least a year old in a matter of days. This meant extra bleach and many washes. Doris and I instructed and helped him beat the clothes on the patio to add age to them.

Martin completed reading the Blue Jackets Manual, and I told him there was certain sections I wanted him to read again, study, and learn thoroughly. These things are the ones that are important and everyone knows them without thinking; things like pay and advancement, leave and liberty, special requests, and shipboard (command) organization.

The routine established by the previous week was broken Tuesday evening when Doris, Martin, and I went to the amusement park. This was in downtown Long Beach in the area of bars, locker clubs, and tattoo parlors.

We enjoyed the rides and games, but we had gone there for a specific purpose. Throughout the evening I quizzed Martin on the rates of the sailors who were also enjoying themselves.

"Chief, I was born and raised in San Diego."

"I realize this, but nevertheless, pay attention to their behavior. You're here to learn. Learn the action of sailors on liberty. Remember this is still study time."

The next evening when I returned from the ship, Martin was in the driveway polishing his car.

"I'm glad to see you took a break." I looked up at the sky and asked, "You wanting it to rain?"

"It probably will. I just finished washing some uniforms so I thought I'd do a little more washing." He pointed to his bucket and said, "We're quite close now."

On the way to dinner, I could also tell he had something else on his mind; and I think I was one step ahead of him. I know a young man of nineteen isn't meant to be cooped up with a book for too long of a period. After our meal, I reached into my wallet, pulled out a twenty dollar bill and asked, "Think you could find some place or someway to spend this?"

He smiled and replied, "Sure could."

I said, "It's a kid-brother type bribe to get you out of the house for the evening."

"I'm sure it is," he said, knowing we were thinking the same thoughts, but beating around the bush with words.

The rest of the week was more study and quizzes. The only new subject introduced was practical small arms. I had checked out from the ship's armory a .45 caliber automatic pistol and a M-1 rifle. He learned the operation and safety mechanisms of both. Saturday morning I gathered the weapons and the ammunition I previously procured. We went to the rifle range to give him a quick indoctrination of their use. The first shot from the M-1 almost set him on his fanny. He commented about the .45 being extremely loud. Learn he did, but a marksman he wasn't.

On our way home from the range, I asked him if he'd like to go home for the rest of the weekend. He nonchalantly agreed he would, and when we arrived at the house he immediately packed the necessities for the overnight stay.

I knew he would have to have gasoline money for the trip so I gave him fifty dollars. After that I told him I would like to have him return relatively early Sunday evening because there were some things I wanted to discuss with him before Monday.

It was near seven-thirty Sunday evening when we heard the sound of Jim's car in the driveway.

As he entered, I asked, "Hungry?"

"Yeh."

"Want a sandwich? Got ham and cheese."

"Great."

"What did your mom and dad have to say?"

"Not much."

"Don't give me that. I'm sure Paul had his two cents worth."

"He did rant and rave somewhat. He says you're crazy. To quote him, he said, 'That guy needs psychiatric treatment. If not treatment, at least consultation.'"

Jimmy did an excellent job of mimicking his dad and we all laughed.

"Of course, he gives Mom a tough time about it too. She fires it right back. She tells him we're doing something that he had always wanted to do but just never had the guts. Oh really, everything is all right. Mom and Dad just like to hear themselves make loud noises."

"Jim, what I wanted to discuss with you is about checking-in aboard the Kreighton. I think you're ready or as ready as you'll ever be. I believe tomorrow morning will be as good a time as any. What do you say?"

"I thought that was why you wanted me to return early this evening. I didn't sleep too well last night thinking about it. I had all sorts of visions. I figured I'm ready if you are . . . and I'm scared. How about you?"

"Yes, I'm scared. Or extremely nervous," I replied. I turned and asked, "How about you, Honey?"

"I've been scared of this thing all along. Tomorrow will be a long day for me."

I'm sure glad everyone agreed with me because I had his orders made up for this date. I went to the bedroom, got his orders and returned.

When I handed them to him he said, "That was sneaky, Chief."

I agreed with a smile.

"Okay. This is the way I've got it mapped out. If there are any questions, bring them up as I go along. This thing is going to be full of 'ifs' until it is finished. The more avenues we explore now, the better our defenses will be."

I explained the outline for tomorrow, and we discussed the "ifs," "ands," "buts," and "maybes" until we were sure of what we were to do. By the time we had everything down pat, it was time to go to bed.

Tomorrow, D. Day . . .

Chapter 10

Near nine o'clock Doris brought Jim to the ship and let him out about 500 feet from the afterbrow. Jim walked up the gangway just as confident as he could possibly be. As he got to the top of the brow, he saluted aft then saluted the Chief of the Watch and said, "James Martin, AZAN reporting for duty, sir."

I made sure Gray was near to meet him. Just as the Chief started to ask him for his orders, Gray interrupted with, "You're Martin aren't you?"

"Yes. Why?" he answered.

"I'm Gray, and we've been expecting you." He turned to the Chief and said, "Chief, I'm from AIMD, and we have advance orders on this guy. I'll be glad to take him down to the Personnel Office if you want."

"All right. Make sure they stamp his arrival time on his orders."

"Sure, Chief. I'll make sure. Come with me, Martin."

They walked down a ladder, through a passageway, and Martin stopped.

"Where are we going? You know good and well I can't go to the Personnel Office."

"I know. Just be patient. We're going to kill some time and later go up to the AIMD Office. Chief Wilson said he'd be there waiting for you. He's been up on the flight deck watching you."

They went down to the lounge, and there they met Whitteker.

Gray introduced them with, "Whitteker, Martin; Martin, Whitteker. Whitteker is in on the whole set up."

"Yeh, I know," Martin replied. "Whitteker and I have already met."

"Hi, Jim. Still scared?"

"You know I am. I think more now than the last time we met. Aren't you?"

Whitteker replied, "Yes!" He unbuttoned a couple of buttons on his shirt, reached inside, and pulled out a card. "Here's your check-in card. May as well get started. It's already signed off by disbursing, medical, and dental. Forged of course."

"Of course."

"Well, you're on your way. Good luck. Gray, why don't you take him by those three places to show him where they are?"

Gray nodded an agreement and said, "See ya, Whit."

Whitteker took a couple steps then turned around and said, "You both realize that Chief Wilson is crazy," paused, and then continued, "and so are we."

With this, they parted company then went around, down, and through what some people may think to be the bowels of the ship. They passed by the places already checked off and went to the aft end of the hangar deck, up the ladder to the Aviation Intermediate Maintenance Department Office.

When they arrived, Martin wasn't surprised to see me present.

Martin was introduced to the Leading Chief first.

"Chief Madson, this is Martin, AZAN. He just checked aboard. We've already checked-in to a few places. Martin, this is Chief Madson, our Leading Chief and this is Chief Wilson, our Avionics Chief."

"Glad to meet you, Martin," I said as I stood and shook his hand after Chief Madson.

"Martin, I want to welcome you aboard the Kreighton and hope you like it here," the Leading Chief stated. "Where did you come from?"

"My last duty station was Pt. Mugu."

"How did you like Mugu?"

"Believe me, I'd rather be there than here," Martin replied.

"You're tense boy. Relax. Chief Wilson here has been bugging me for an AZ to work for him in Avionics. As of right now, I think that's where you'll be assigned. Chief, why don't you take Martin and show him around? Show him your office and see if he wants to work for you."

"I'll be glad to. Come with me, Martin. We'll get some more checking-in done while we look around."

As we walked to the door, I looked over at Gray. I could see he was trying to ignore us yet could hardly keep from laughing out loud.

Chief Madson had accompanied us to the door, and he also noticed Gray's attitude. "What's the matter with you?" he growled toward Gray.

"Nothing, Chief. Nothing. I was thinking about something that happened a couple of months ago."

Martin and I walked out the door and down the ladder onto the hangar deck.

"How's it going?" I asked.

"Pretty good and I was relieved a little when Chief Madson said I was going to work for you."

"We discussed it earlier and were just waiting for the next AZ to report aboard. I think I kind of had the edge on him knowing who and when that would be. I try to take cinches, not chances."

We walked forward on the hangar deck, and I pointed out different things as we walked. As we neared the Quarterdeck, I explained the function of all that was visible. From there we went to the legal office. Another check-in.

Next we went back to the hangar deck, and when we arrived abreast of the Master At Arms Office, I said, "Let's check-in with the master at arms then we'll go to the PAO. Follow the leader," I said jokingly.

When we arrived in the Public Affairs Office, the yeoman gave Jim some preprinted forms to fill out. When he finished, he handed them back to the yeoman.

He replied, "That's it. We'll see to it that a news release of your new duty station gets published in your home town newspaper."

My heart leaped into my throat. I was sure Martin was in the same frame of mind until he said, "If I have a choice, I'd rather you wouldn't." Once again his composure astonished me. I was sure I had picked the right man.

"Well, if that's the way you want it," the yeoman said as he tore up the papers and threw them in the trashcan. He signed the check-in card without hesitation.

We continued the check-in process and his indoctrination of the layout of the ship. During our travels, we arrived at the division berthing compartment.

"Welcome to your bedroom, Martin," I said laughingly.

"I'm unimpressed," he replied as his eyes scanned the berths. "They stack us four high on a bunk made of canvas laced onto an aluminum frame, give us a three inch mattress, and want us to rest comfortably."

As his eyes continued searching the compartment and making reference to the two-foot cube lockers, he asked, "How many of those nutshells do I get to store my gear in?"

"One," interrupted a sarcastic voice, "and lucky you, you get that top rack. It'll be nice and warm when we get to South East Asia."

"Martin, this is Baker, ADJ3. He's the PPO, Police Petty Officer. That's to say it's his job to maintain the cleanliness of this space and the head. It's also his responsibility to assign racks and lockers, hold reveille, and make sure taps is observed. He's the cop. See his badge?"

I continued, "Baker, this is Martin, AZAN. He just checked aboard this morning."

They exchanged their greetings, and Martin discovered Baker was serious in assigning him the top rack. He was also assigned a locker, and Martin stated he would be back later in the day to store his gear.

"Your mattress cover, blanket, pillow, and pillow cover will be on your rack by the time you get back. I want that rack made up properly just as soon as possible. If you don't know how, look at the other racks and follow suit. If you aren't in your rack, I want it squared away at all times. Do you read me?"

Martin replied, "Right."

We departed to continue checking-in.

Martin followed me back down to the hangar deck and when we arrived I said, "Don't let Baker scare you. He likes to harass people, but on the other hand, don't give him any guff. He'll put you on report faster than you can blink and the first thing you know . . . Well, let's just say we can't afford to have that happen."

We walked around on the hangar deck for a while and wandered up to the flight deck. His education of the practical Navy grew. I escorted him back to the AIMD Office.

"Gray, how about you taking Martin up to the compartment so he can store his gear, square away his bunk, get
out of those whites, and then to chow? Martin, I'll see you
back here at 1300. That's when we'll tour the Avionic spaces.
Also, I want to introduce you to your division officer."

Martin picked up his gear and they departed. I stepped
on into the Leading Chief's office and said, "I think that
guy is going to be all right."

"Fine," Madson replied. "Let's get some chow."

Later, when Martin returned from chow he approached me and asked, "May I see you alone for a
minute, Chief Wilson?"

"Sure, Martin," I replied. "Let's step outside."

As we left the department office, I knew he had already
hit a stumbling block. How could a guy possibly get into
any sort of a jam by changing his clothes and going to chow?
Then it hit me. He couldn't have changed his mind. No!
Tell me that isn't it. What could it be?

"Why are you always doing that to me?"

"What? What are you talking about, Martin."

"Every time we part company, you kick me in the
teeth. That's what."

"You're not making sense. You'd better start this thing
at the beginning."

"Just before I went to chow, you said for me to meet
you here and that you were going to introduce me to the
division officer. That's what. You know I could hardly eat?
It wasn't bad enough for me to be on the edge of a breakdown this morning; you give me something more to worry
me while I'm trying to eat. This happened Saturday just
before I went home. You said, 'Come back early, I have something to discuss before Monday.' Well, I worried about that
the rest of the day Saturday and all day Sunday. I'm going to

have a nervous breakdown before the day is out. I have passed the point of being scared. I'm terrified!"

"Okay! Okay! Ease up! From now on, I won't give you any sort of warning. We've got a couple more things to do then I'll find a reason to get us both off early. Doris won't mind us coming home early. I'm sure she's quite worried. Remember how she was the last time? Now, are you sure you want it that way?"

"Yes, I am," he said emphatically.

"All right, let's go back inside."

We walked back inside and over to Gray's desk.

"Gray, I want you to type up a liberty card for Martin. I've talked to Chief Madson, Martin is going to work for me, and he's to be put into the second section. Just as soon as you get it typed, bring it in, and I'll ask the Commander to sign it."

I turned to Martin. "Come with me. I'll take you in and introduce you to the Maintenance Officer."

Before he had a chance to think about it, I knocked and we stepped into the Commander's office.

"Commander, this is Martin, the AZAN who checked-in this morning. Martin, this is Commander Franklin, our department officer and the ship's aviation Maintenance Officer.

"Welcome aboard, Martin. They tell me you're from Mugu."

"Yes, sir," he replied in a semi-choked voice.

"We're glad to have you. Ever been stationed aboard ship before?"

"No sir," Martin responded weakly.

"How did you like Mugu?" the Commander questioned.

"Fine, sir."

The Commander came back with a couple more leading questions, but before Martin could reply, Gray walked in with the liberty card.

"Excuse me, Commander," I interrupted. "Martin has completed the majority of his checking-in and has told me he wants to open a bank account before they close this afternoon. If it's all right with you, I'd like to take off also, and I'll drive Martin to the bank."

"It's all right with me," he said as I handed him Martin's liberty card. "Better check with Bill before you leave."

"Yes, sir, I will. I've got a couple of things to wrap up before I go."

The Commander signed the liberty card and handed it to Martin and said, "Glad to have you here, Martin. Again, welcome aboard."

They shook hands and we walked out of the office.

Martin asked, "Who's this "Bill" you have to check with?"

"That's our Division Officer, Lieutenant Carter."

I followed that with, "Change back into your whites, and I'll meet you on the hangar deck near the afterbrow, the gangway, in about twenty minutes. This time, you are on your own. No escort."

We started to part and then I called him back. "Jim. I hated to do that to you a while ago, but you were the one that said 'no warning.' Remember?"

He gave me a look, and we parted. I walked off smiling for I knew the worst for him was over. An introduction to the division officer and that would be it. From then on, it would be a daily survival.

Jim met me as previously planned, but was quiet all the way home. I didn't know if he was angry with me or with the scheme. I didn't bother questioning him. I was sure he could make his own decisions.

When we arrived Doris came running out to the car. She was anxious to hear the proceedings of the day. Jim acknowledged her presence, and went ahead of us into the house.

"What's the matter with him?" she asked.

"He's had a rough morning. Scared half to death, and I wasn't of much help."

I started the story from the beginning. We walked into the house, and I continued the story as she fixed me a drink. Just about the time I finished the story, Jim walked out of the bedroom, a bag in hand, and headed toward the front door.

"Where do you think you're going?" I said in an exploding tone.

Just as calm as he could be, he replied, "San Diego."

Since he was calm, I decided to remain calm and asked, "What time will you be back?"

"Don't know," he replied and walked out the door.

"Do you think he will be back?" Doris asked.

"I don't know, but I imagine he will. He's gone through a lot today. Remember how he drove off the day I asked him to join my, er, our scheme. It's as much yours as mine. Anyhow, I think driving and thinking is his method of meditation. Maybe he enjoys being alone while he makes important decisions."

Doris said, "You know, I went through a bit of mental torment myself. I expected you to call me at lunchtime. You could have let me know how things were going. However, now that the day of reckoning is finished . . . with official trouble . . . I feel as though it's time to relax. And, while I'm thinking about it, I got my invitation to play in the tournament at Pebble Beach in two months. Right now I really have mixed emotions. I'm nervous over you and Jim, and I'm excited about Pebble Beach. I've a lot of practice to get in between now and then, and maybe I can get my mind off 'the scheme,' as you put it."

In answer to her mentioning it's time to relax, I had said, "I agree."

In answer to her invitation, I had said, "That's wonderful."

When she finished talking, I said, "With Jim gone and the rest of the afternoon off, relaxing was not totally what I had in mind."

She replied, "Want to race to the shower?"

I smiled, and she ran out of the room.

Chapter 11

That evening Doris and I went to a movie and from there to a cocktail lounge. As we sipped our drinks, there seem to be a solemn atmosphere between us.

"Something wrong?" I asked.

"Yes, there is. However, I think it's too late to talk about it."

"What do you mean?"

"This scheme, Jack, I think it's gone too far. When you first came up with the idea, I went along and sort of patronized you. I shouldn't have. Now I'm sorry that I did. Maybe I should say I'm frightened of the whole thing. At first, I didn't believe you would go through with it, and I was sure no one else would go along with you. I was positive it would fall through. That's why I never revolted. Every day I gave it more thought. Today, I fully realized what was happening. While you and Jim were on that ship, I was scared to death. I have tried not to show it, but I just can't hold back any longer. Maybe Paul was right."

"Your attitude sure seems to have changed since noon."

"While you were sleeping earlier, I got to thinking about it. The scheme. Your career. My career. I got to thinking, just what are we doing? Jack, we are on the brink of possibly ruining our lives along with others. I am scared, excited, depressed, and confused."

"Honey, I'm scared too. We all are. Jim, Whitteker, Gray. All of us are scared. Even Paul. There's a risk involved but I'm sure, no, I'm positive, we can go through with it."

"But Jack, can't you see. You're putting our whole lives into the hands of a nineteen-year-old boy. His immaturity came to light today when he walked out the door. Will this happen again? We can't afford for it to happen again."

"Honey, I know you're right in a way but . . . . Well, I just can't put into words of how positive I am there will be no trouble, and I do have confidence in Jim. He was upset today just as you are. Darling, have the same confidence in me that I have in Jim. When I get to the point where I lack confidence in myself or I see that something drastic is going to happen I'll have Whitteker forge some orders and we will get Martin off the ship. Okay?"

She didn't reply. She bowed her head and covered her eyes with her hand. She refused to look at me.

We finished our drinks in silence and departed. My stomach let me know that one drink was enough.

I still had the taste of the antacid tablet in my mouth as we arrived home just after midnight. We looked at each other as we noticed Jim's car in the drive. We parked along side and went in.

Just as we entered, Jim greeted us just as though nothing had happened and introduced us to an unexpected guest.

"Mrs. Wilson, Jack, I'd like to introduce Janet DeVarnes. Janet, this is Mr. and Mrs. Wilson." We exchanged our greeting and Jim continued. "Janet and I are engaged."

I was at a loss for words; I was astounded and yet furious. I thought, "She knows, her parents know. Everyone knows Jim is going to be a stowaway. Maybe Doris is right. Give this thing up before it gets completely out of hand." Rather than get excited and blow my top, I listened.

Jim said, "Maybe I'd better explain. Janet and I are planning on getting married. Not in the near future. We've discussed marriage and have tried to approach it in a mature aspect. We realize we're not financially able and well, just too young also. So we have decided that I would finish college as Mom and Dad, and we want. We decided we would make more definite plans as time goes by. That's a rough background. Then you came along with your stowaway scheme.

"By Dad's actions and yours, I saw how serious you were. The decision was mine. Yet it wasn't. Janet and I had made plans also. I didn't want to say yes or no without consulting her. I wanted to say yes, but felt as though I didn't have the right. So I left the house and drove over to see her and to discuss it with her.

"There are more reasons as to why I wanted to join you in a hoax against the service, but this isn't the time to explain. Right now, I want to explain how she enters the picture.

"I drove over to her house on the day you first asked me to join you. To make a long story short, we discussed the scheme, and I convinced her that all would go well. Last Saturday, I reassured her everything was going to be all right.

"Today? Well, today I was nervous, excited, angry, and struck back at you for my shortcomings. As I drove to San Diego this afternoon I realized that, and I went to Janet's house. I haven't been home. I brought Janet back up here with me tonight to meet you, to explain some of my background problems, and to drive my car back to San Diego. I won't need it anymore for nearly a year.

"Her using it and taking care of it would be better than letting it set idle while we are at sea. Her parents won't like it, but there are a lot of things in this world that we don't like. That's about it in a nutshell."

I asked, "Janet, do your parents know about you and Jim being, well, informally engaged?"

"Yes, Mr. Wilson, they do."

"Do they know what kind of a scheme Jim is involved in?"

"Not exactly. They know that he is going away for almost a year. You see, they think we're too young to be as serious as we are about marriage. They think this will be an opportunity for me to either forget him or to see if I'm still positive about him at a later date. You know, the out of sight out of mind routine. They have no idea of where he is going or what he will be doing."

"Do you know? Do you know what risks and consequences surround what Jim and I are doing?"

"Yes I do. Jim has explained it to me as you have explained it to him. I am also aware of the confidential requirement."

"Good. You see, I've run into another problem. Doris isn't positive now that we can go through with it. She's scared.

"And I might add, she definitely has the right to be. She's in the LPGA and made quite a name for herself. She too, has a career.

"Jim, from now on, the rest of this is in your hands. Our fate, Doris,' mine, yours, Janet's, Gray's and Whitteker's, lies in your hands. I have proved one point to myself and that is I could get you on board. The rest of the scheme is no longer mine. It's yours.

"Doris thinks we should stop now. I could get you a set of orders transferring you off. That would be the end of it. What do you think?"

"Chief, there were some other reasons as to why I wanted to go along with this. Again, I say I'd rather not mention them now. To answer your question, I think we should go on. Mrs. Wilson, trust me."

Doris nodded a reluctant approval and asked, "Janet, do your parents know where you are?"

"Not exactly."

"Let's call them and tell them that you're spending the night with some friends of the Martin family who live in Long Beach. If necessary, I'll talk with your mother and convince her all is well and that you will be home tomorrow. I don't want you to drive that distance this late at night. I'm sure you're already tired."

I said, "Jim, you inherit the couch tonight. While Janet and Doris phone, you get your necessary uniforms out of your bedroom. Also, why don't you suggest to Janet and Doris to ask about Janet staying longer. Tomorrow evening we could take in Disneyland."

"Great idea. I'll see about that now," he enthusiastically replied.

Jim got the date settled, and we retired for the hour was nearing 2 AM.

Chapter 12

When I woke Jim at six, he was quite reluctant to get up. My perseverance had him up and in uniform with a cup of coffee in him by seven o'clock. We arrived at the ship, and Jim went through the necessary ritual at the afterbrow. He showed his ID card and liberty card, saluted, and requested permission to come aboard. There was no hesitation. He executed the whole thing as if it were from habit.

"You go up to the compartment, change into dungarees, and meet me in the department office. From there we'll go up to the division office for muster. See you shortly."

"Right, Chief," he answered with an accent on Chief and departed smiling.

It appeared as though it was going to be a good day.

I went into the department office, poured myself a cup of coffee and read the "Plan-of-the-Day." Chief Madson and I had hardly started a conversation when Martin came in.

"Good morning, Martin. How are you?" the Leading Chief inquired.

"Just fine, Chief," Martin replied.

He had no more than finished his sentence when the Commander came in.

"Good morning, Martin, Chief Wilson, and of course you too," the Commander said cynically and directed the latter portion of his greeting to Chief Madson.

We acknowledged with a near simultaneous, "Good morning, Commander."

Just as Martin and I started for the door, Gray came in and greeted us with a good morning. We acknowledged and departed.

On the way up to the Avionics Office, Martin commented, "Everybody seems over-friendly. Makes me feel as though they know something."

"You've got a guilty conscience is all." I said this jokingly and we laughed about it the rest of the way to the Avionics Shop.

The morning muster was uneventful and after introducing Martin to rest of the crew, I gave him a tour of the electronic shops and the electric shop. I explained what type of work each shop accomplished and how he would have to know some of their functions.

I explained to him that we are also responsible for the passageways around the shops and the office. In this light, we are responsible for their cleanliness, painting, and care. I assured him that he would be getting his fair share of cleaning. And of course, swabbing. Every Friday morning was to be field day and that he would be properly assigned.

From there we went into the Avionics Office, and I introduced Martin to Lieutenant Carter.

"Glad to have you aboard, Martin," the Lieutenant remarked. "I hope you will be able to take care of some of the work around the office. Chief Wilson keeps telling me how much work there is for an AZ to do around here. Frankly, I think he exaggerates so if you can take care of enough of the work to keep him off my back, I'll be happy. Incidentally, I am the welfare and recreation officer so there will be occasional jobs that I will be asking you to do for me along that line. You do type don't you?"

"Yes, sir, I do"

"Otherwise, Chief Wilson runs the show. That is to say, what he says, goes. All your work will be for him in this office excluding your duty nights on which you'll be required to stand a watch called department duty yeoman. You'll have to have Gray or one of the other yeomen down there give you a check out on that job. Occasionally I'll want a cup of coffee. Hope you don't mind a little waiter work. Some days you'll want a few hours off early and occasionally a day off. Remember this on the waiter work routine. To make the coffee easy, I drink it black.

"Don't get into trouble and don't give anyone a hard time. Do your work well and we'll get along fine. Now, is there anything I can do for you?"

"No, sir. Nothing I can think of. Chief Wilson has seen to most of my wants and needs."

"Okay. Chief Wilson, from here on, he's yours. Again, Martin, glad to have you aboard," Lieutenant Carter concluded.

"Martin still has some checking-in to do," I interjected. "We'll get that finished off this morning, and he has his bunk and locker to square away. I won't get much out of him today, so I won't start him on his duties here in the office until tomorrow."

Lieutenant Carter said, "What ever you say, Chief. He's yours."

With that, I introduced him to the calibration technicians, and we left the office to finish the check-in process.

"Lieutenant Carter seems to be a pretty good guy," Martin stated.

"As a matter of fact, he is," I replied. "He gives me a free wheel in running the division. He's generally up to his neck in that welfare/recreation mess. Treat him right, Jim. He's worth it, and it may pay off in dividends in the event we ever need them."

"I get what you mean, Chief."

We finished the checking-in process, and I showed him more of the layout of the ship. From there, we went back to the department office and reported the conclusion of it to the Leading Chief. He asked Gray to take Martin to the personnel office and turn in the check-in card.

"I can find it and turn the card in myself, Chief," Martin interjected.

"Chief, I'd like to take a break and go with him if you don't mind," said Gray. "Also, Martin is going to have to stand these watches down here, and there are a few things I'd like to discuss with him."

"Fine," he said. "Wilson, how about you? I am going below to the mess for a cup of coffee."

"Sold," I replied, and we too departed shortly behind Gray and Martin.

While we were in the Chiefs' Mess, Chief Madson commented, "Seems as though you've found a fine young lad in Martin."

"That he appears to be. How good of an AZ or worker he will be remains to be seen." I replied and then repeated, "How good he is remains to be seen."

"How long have you known him?"

"I met him yesterday morning when he checked-in."

"Horse manure!"

"Just what does that mean?"

"Jack, the kid looks to you and at you, as if you were his daddy."

"Not me, baby!"

"Maybe that's it. Maybe he is looking to you to be his daddy. Do you reckon the kid is a little, well-you-know-what?"

"Hadn't even given it a thought. I'd say no. Doris and I have never wanted kids and therefore, never had any. I don't know how a kid would look at his daddy. That could be the reason you recognized it. I'm sure the kid just found somebody that he could look up to." I smiled as I said, "Maybe that's it and you don't recognize it. Did you ever have anybody look up to you?"

The Leading Chief came back with, "Let's get out of here and get some work done. Let's see if we can do something constructive about getting this ship out to sea."

Chapter 13

While driving home at the end of the second day, I asked Jim how things went for him without my looking over his shoulder.

"Well, I've got my bunk and locker squared away. Now let me tell you, trying to make up a bed nearly eight feet in the air is, without a doubt, tough.

"I spent most of the day with Gray. Talked to Whitteker this morning. I do have something in common with those two.

"Also, I put my check-in card in a drawer in the Avionics Office. Gray told me you have a file that you would want to keep it in. He told me it was your blackmail file."

I laughed and said, "If anyone should know about my blackmail file, he and Whitteker are the two who should know."

When we arrived at home, Doris and Janet were in the driveway awaiting our arrival.

"Well now, don't you look handsome in a uniform," Janet commented to Jim. "This is something I never expected to see. What does the green stripes mean? What is that thing above the stripes mean? Also what is that ribbon?"

"A; don't get smart. B; I think the Chief can tell you more about the green stripes and uniform stuff and C; don't I get a kiss? I'm sure Mr. and Mrs. Wilson have seen young people kiss."

She replied, "I've never kissed a sailor. Do you really think I should? If there's any one thing my daddy has warned me about, it's kissing sailors."

She reluctantly kissed him and blushed a bit.

"Mrs. Wilson, do you have a camera?" Janet asked. "I would like to have a picture of Jim in his uniform."

"Yes Janet, I do. Stay here and I'll bring it right out," Doris replied as she ran off into the house.

I could tell by the actions of the two women that they had hit it off quite well. They seemed to have become instant friends.

When Doris came out, she stated that there were only three pictures yet to be taken on the roll. She took a picture of Jim, a picture of Jim and Janet together, and a picture of Jim and I.

With that finished, she took the roll of film out of the camera and we went into the house.

I fixed myself a drink. While I was doing so, Doris gave me a slightly disgusted look, so I added a little more water.

"Jack, I've asked Janet if she would like to come up and spend some time with me while you two are at sea. She has accepted the invitation on a when-she-has-the-time basis."

Our voices became louder as I went into the bedroom and changed clothes. I made it a quick change.

"Another thing that you two have agreed upon is that we are going out to eat tonight. Right?" I asked from the bedroom.

"As a matter of fact, we did discuss it to some extent," she loudly replied.

I had returned just in time to catch her as she turned to Janet and winked.

"I know you did. Here it is time to eat and you haven't made any preparation to eat at home. I'll concede before you even ask. Would you rather eat on the way to Disneyland, at Disneyland, or on the way back home?"

Janet said, "At Disneyland. It's too early to eat now and part of the entertainment of Disneyland is the eating of the junk food." She turned to Doris and winked.

I had watched both of them throughout the conversation and knew that the whole thing had been prearranged and Jim and I were nothing but cattle being led to the feminine slaughter. When a man is up against two conniving women, he doesn't have a chance, and that's it!

I finished my drink. Jim and Janet went outside to be alone while Doris made last minute arrangements to her hair.

Doris and I were ready to go, and we walked out of the house hand in hand as we had seen Jim and Janet do.

When we got outside, Jim and Janet were still kissing, as, I guess, teenagers should do. However, I was forced to interrupt.

"Martin, there is no way in this world that I'm going to go to Disneyland with a sailor. Get on some civvies."

Of course this broke up the kiss and Janet said to Jim, "Martin? Does he always call you Martin?"

Jim nodded his head and said, "Affirmative. He's got me answering to names like sailors, looking like a sailor, and even talking like a sailor. The next thing you know, he will probably have me chasing pretty girls like sailors do."

With that Janet feigned a slap. Jim stopped it with a grasp of her wrist, gave her a peck of a kiss, and ran back into the house.

Disneyland was great. It seems as though a person never sees all of it. Doris and I have been there several times and there's always something new, something we have not seen, or something we have not done. We love it. It's fabulous, ever new and ever changing. It's exciting, exhausting, and yet relaxing. It takes your mind off this world the minute you step through the gate. We enjoy it as much as teenagers do. Even as a much as preteens. It's truly an indescribable place.

This night of amusement was started early and ended early for Janet had to drive to San Diego. When we arrived at the house, Jim and Janet had a few minutes alone. Janet called her mother to let her know she was starting home and should arrive in about two hours.

I insisted on an early retirement due to the late hours of last night, the excitement, and exhaustion of tonight. I had given Jim and Janet some time alone outside and when I heard Jim's car drive off, I walked outside.

Jim was standing alone watching as she drove off. I interrupted his solitude, and we stood outside talking for a while. My insistence upon an early retirement had been shot.

Chapter 14

The beginning of the third day was routine. After muster, I commenced showing Martin his duties as an Aviation Administrationman. He was eager to learn and wanted to get started on each item I showed him. I had to hold him back. I didn't want him to set the world on fire. Indoctrination and instructions occupied the morning, and in the afternoon I assigned him to holding inventory on all the technical publications we had on file in the office and making sure they were filed in alpha/numerical sequence. This assignment would hold him over for a couple of days.

That evening I went home alone. Jim had the duty and would have to remain on board overnight. It also gave Doris and I a night to ourselves. This would be our first completely free night in almost three weeks.

As Doris and I were eating, she told me Dolly had called and asked how things were going. She said she assured Dolly everything was going real well and that Jim was doing fine. As she was telling me of the phone conversation, I was thinking "That's mothers for you, constantly worrying about their offspring."

After we had finished eating, again I was thinking about mothers. How mothers worry about their little boys who go off to the service. Little boys? They are men. Leave them alone. They can take care of themselves. Uncle Sam won't hurt them. They may find themselves involved in the shaping of the United States.

I was really getting my "bitters against mothers" worked up when the phone rang.

"Hello," I snapped.

"Hello, Jack?" the other voice asked.

I didn't recognize the voice. "Yes, this is Jack," I replied somewhat calm.

"Paul Martin here. Is Jim there?"

"No he isn't, Paul. He's aboard ship. Is there anything in particular you wanted? Do you need to talk to him?"

"Not really. Just wanted to find out how things are going. You know Dolly is a little worried. I thought I'd call to make sure everything is all right."

"You're not worried about him are you, Paul?"

"Not me. I'm sure Jim can take care of himself and even if he couldn't, I know he's in good hands. However, I just wanted to call to keep Dolly cooled. You know how mothers are."

"Paul, did Dolly ask you to call?" I inquired.

"Well, er, yes she did. Well, she hinted that I call."

"Is Dolly there now, Paul?"

"No, she isn't. She went shopping with a neighbor. Why do you ask?"

"No reason. I just thought she might want to say hello to Doris while we are on the line and being they haven't talked to each other in some time.

"Paul, you can assure Dolly everything is fine. I might also add that Jim probably won't be home until the weekend after this one. He'll fill you in on the happenings at that time."

"Thanks, Jack. Bye now."

"Good bye, Paul."

I placed the phone back on the receiver and had myself a good laugh. Mothers! Mothers? Fathers!

"Who were you talking to that gave you such a good laugh?" Doris asked. "I thought you were talking to Paul Martin but listening to your side of the conversation it sounded a little strange if you were talking to him."

"It was Paul. Mother Paul Martin," I said and then I related my previous thoughts and the whole phone conversation.

After our laughter had subsided, I grabbed Doris and gave her a good hard kiss.

"What was that for?"

"That was for not being a mother."

After that kiss, I gave her another kiss.

"I know what that kiss was for," she stated. "It wasn't at all like the last. How about another one?"

Chapter 15

Again it was time to get underway. The ship was to participate in exercises just off the coast of California and was to be out for only a week. This would be an excellent introductory cruise for Martin.

As Martin and I stood on the flight deck and watched the ship move slowly away from the pier, I could tell he was filled with anticipation. He would make comments on items which were either common place or insignificant to me.

He effectively dragged me from one point of the ship to another, and as the last tug cast off he and I were standing on the fantail watching the shipyard disappear into the background. I studied his facial expressions and comments. I concluded that here was a young man who has lost everything; his whole world was drifting away.

Rather than belittle or tease him at this moment, I made the comment we should return to the office. There was work to be done.

Our second morning out was interrupted by the 1MC with "This is a drill, this is a drill. General quarters, all hands man your battle stations." These words were spoken over the blaring of the GQ alarm. My general quarters station was in the Avionics Shop and Martin's was in repair seven.

"What do I do now, Chief?" Martin asked.

"Among the things I've given you is a card which tells you what to do. Rather, it tells you where to go. Your general quarters station is repair seven which is aft on the hangar deck. Proceed to that area by going down and aft on the port side of the ship or up and forward on the starboard side. It's just as you read in the Blue Jackets Manual. In your case, you take the former. As far aft on the starboard side of the hangar deck as you can go, is a repair locker. There will be a Chief there named Wallace. He's in charge and will teach you all there is to do while at GQ. Scared?"

"Yeah. Well, not scared. I'm as nervous as I have ever been!"

"Okay. Play this as cool and as confident as you have everything else, and all will go fine. Above all, don't be afraid to tell Chief Wallace that you don't know what to do. He'll help you. Just be the actor that you've been so far and think of Chief Wallace as your acting coach. You've got to learn these things so you may a well get it in your head and when you want to learn, it makes it easier."

I let the guys in the electronics shop know I wouldn't be there during GQ, and I tried to accompany Martin to his station. The movement was quite frantic throughout the ship, and in the scramble Martin and I got separated. However, he made it to the proper spot just a few steps ahead of me. I introduced Martin to the Chief and explained this was Martin's first ship, first cruise, and of course, his first GQ.

Even though I knew I could be of no assistance, I stood nearby and watched.

Chief Wallace efficiently organized the men and instructed them that this was an introductory GQ. He outlined the duties and responsibilities of that particular repair party. He demonstrated the use, care, and importance of the Oxygen Breathing Apparatus commonly known as an OBA. It had been some time since I had used one, so I volunteered myself as a model for the demonstration. I knew this would also ease the tension that Martin was experiencing.

After each man tried on the OBA, Chief Wallace continued with his lecture of the responsibilities and the duties of the repair party. He was still in the process of demonstrating a piece of equipment when the secure from general quarters sounded. Martin and I returned to the office, and he related his thoughts and emotions of his first general quarters.

"Well, you know I was scared. My heart was pounding most of the time we were there. By the way, thanks for baby-sitting me through the first one. Well, like I say, I was scared. I was thinking of all the general quarters that I've seen in the movies and on television. I was thinking if this were war, really war, what would I do? Would I be scared? Yes. Yes, I would be scared. If in the event it was war, or even if it wasn't a drill, I'm sure I would be scared then also. What I kept saying to myself was, 'Act.' This is a drill, and this is a chance to learn, and above all, act. Act. Act with confidence.

"When it came my turn to try on the OBA, I said to myself, 'Chief Wilson did it, so can you.' Well, like you said, play it cool and be an actor. I tried, but I knew good and well that I was going to suffocate while I had that thing on my head.

"I kept saying to myself, 'Keep cool. Act.' Really, everything did go quite well and I didn't suffocate. I just don't think I would like to go through that for real, but I have the confidence in myself that I could do it."

While he was relating this to me I got lost in what he was saying and found myself watching his enthusiasm and my confidence in him grew.

"You know, Chief? I'm positive I could do all the things Chief Wallace said would be required of me."

I assured him these were normal reactions and everyone experiences them. The only time that it gets real exciting is when the alarm is not preceded by, "This is a drill." This is a drill."

"Not only will you be going through general quarters drills, you will be going through man overboard drills and fire-fighting drills. That is, during your GQ you will be fighting fires without fires. Some will even involve aircraft and pilot rescue. You will also simulate ammunition fires. Naturally this will involve first aid and self aid. The part that makes you feel like a dummy is when you are the dummy. You know that sometime, someday you will be picked as the victim."

By this time, we had worked our way back up to the Avionics Shop and again our day settled down to a normal routine excluding the times Martin took a break to look at the ocean. I went topside with him a couple of times and was thankful for a calm sea.

We were standing in a catwalk looking out across the ocean when he said, "You know, Chief? It is hard to realize just how big this ocean is. Both. It is really big, and it is hard to realize that.

"I've seen the ocean in the movies, on television, and of course, from the beach. Now, here, it just doesn't seem the same."

The next day brought what I am sure Jim was anticipating. While we were working in the office, a loud crash was heard coming from overhead. A whining sort of scream followed this.

Jim looked up at me, and I knew what was on his mind before he spoke.

"If you want to see what it was, come with me to Vultures Row. We may as well get it over with right now," I said.

I took him through some passageways and up ladders. We soon arrived at the 09 level. This was five decks above the flight deck in the superstructure where a spectator can clearly view flight operations without getting in the way of anyone.

As we arrived, a plane was on its final portion of the landing pattern. It was quite crowded, but we managed to get a good view. The plane came in smooth and uneventful.

That was the way I saw it. Jim said it was a controlled crash. Its wheels did crash onto the flight deck as the tail hook caught one of the cross deck pendants. The cable paid out with an unmistakable whine, and the plane came to smooth yet abrupt stop.

I explained to him the plane was called an A4 and was probably the smallest of the jet aircraft the Navy has. I again explained to him we were an Anti-Submarine carrier and the squadrons that would be going overseas with us were a couple of squadron of the A4's, but most would be helicopters. Another one of the exceptions was the ship's own plane. It's called a COD, short for Carrier On board Delivery. I told him in an emergency, other planes might have to come to us for landing. I also explained these guys were just going through carrier qualifications and would be practicing this extensively while on this cruise.

As I was talking, a man from the arresting gear crew went out toward the plane, made sure the arresting cable was free, and off the tail hook. He gave a signal and was running back to the catwalk as the cable took up its former position, and the plane taxied forward out of the landing pattern.

Seven planes in all came aboard. After the last landed the planes were catapulted off, one by one and then the procedure repeated itself.

When the first plane came back for a landing, it came in too high and had to take a wave off.

I'd seen enough. The noise from the jet engines, the wind in the face and too much standing had gotten to me. A little of that goes a long way and is more than enough for me.

For Martin, the excitement prevailed, and I gave him permission to stay. I had other work to do. After I got away from the noise, it seemed as though I were in a different world. I just couldn't see why anyone would want work or could work in such an environment. It made me appreciate my nice, quiet, cozy, air conditioned office and electronic shops.

That evening after dark as I wandered around the ship, I saw Martin sitting alone on one of the sponsons. I stood back and watched him for about fifteen minutes. Again, I knew what he was thinking. Three days at sea, and he had experienced the excitement of general quarters, viewed flight operations, and now he had found a minute to be alone with his thoughts.

Many thoughts drift through a man's mind while alone staring at the vacant dark sea. Most generally the thoughts are of loved ones and how they are missed. It is truly a lonely feeling.

I didn't disturb him and walked away leaving him alone with his thoughts.

Chapter 16

The phone rang. It was Martin.

I shouted, "You get up here right now," and slammed the phone down. A minor thing such as getting out of bed at reveille, and he blows it. If there is any one thing I need is for this whole mess to fall apart over something so minor.

As Martin walked in through the door, I started ranting, raving, and cursing. I carried on for what seemed like thirty minutes, and then I stormed out the door myself. I hardly gave him a chance to explain. Hardly? I never gave him any chance.

I went straight to the berthing compartment to find Baker, the Police Petty Officer. I wanted to get the whole story from him. He was the one who had held reveille and put Martin on report. I had to stop the report chit and this was the best place to start. I realized if a man doesn't get up at reveille it is Baker's job to report it, but I just couldn't afford for it to be Martin.

My composure was near normal when I approached Baker and said, "I hear one of my boys didn't make it up on time this morning."

"That's right, Chief," he replied.

"Would you mind giving me the whole story?"

Baker explained Martin just didn't get up on time. He turned on the lights at 0600 and shook all the racks. From there, he went to the other berthing compartment that AIMD occupied and held reveille in it. He said he went to the department office, made a pot of coffee, and returned to the first berthing compartment. The time was 0642. Martin was still in his rack so he shook the rack, woke Martin, and put him on report.

"Then there was no incident? Martin never gave you any guff or rebuked in any type of manner or method?"

"No, Chief, he didn't."

"Do you think it is necessary that a report chit be made out on him for this incident?"

"I sure do, Chief. This is my routine course of action, and it maintains my authority. If I had no authority or some sort of big stick, no one would get up on time. You can see if I can't maintain some sort of authority, there is no need for me to even be here. I could be working back down in the shop working in my rate and at least accomplishing something."

"I realize this, but this isn't what I'm trying to say. A portion of the intent for putting a man on report is for correction or to remedy a situation. To take him to mast over something this trivial is surely not necessary."

"Trivial?" he shouted. "I just told you the necessity of my putting a man on report, and you say, trivial?"

"Maybe I chose the wrong word. In your opinion the wrong word, but I didn't come down here to play word games. I want the report chit stopped. It's the young man's first incident, and I can't see the necessity of the report chit. If you won't stop it, I'll go to Chief Madson. I can't make you stop the chit, so I'm asking you. But I do want you to know what my intentions are, and I'm sure I can get it stopped somewhere up the line. I think it would save face for you if you stopped it rather than my going over your head."

Right there I was playing my own cards. If this ever happened again, I would still have my influence with the Leading Chief. I couldn't see burning my ace in the hole over this one.

"Now Baker, I'm asking you. Are you going to stop the chit or do you want me to go up the ladder? It's your choice."

"I don't want to stop it. I don't think it is right, but I am not so dumb to know how thick you Chiefs are. Being you're asking, I will. Now I want you to know something. I think you owe me, and believe me, I won't be bashful about asking for repayment."

The Navy is such a close knit organization it's very important you know who your friends are and it's always very nice to have influence in the right place at the right time. Also it's equally important to know who not to cross.

"Understood, and, by the way, thanks."

From the berthing compartment I went straight to the Department Office. As I walked in, I gave my usual good morning greetings to all present and walked over to Gray's desk. Softly I said, "I want to talk to you. In private." I faked a smile and walked out the door knowing Gray would be a few steps behind me.

When he came out, I asked, "Do you know what happened this morning?"

"No. What?"

"Martin was put on report." His eyes bugged as he gasped, and his chin fell.

I continued, "Baker put him on report for sleeping in. Now there is no need for me to go through a long explanation of what this means. I will tell you I talked Baker into stopping the chit and we, this includes you, can't afford this. I hate to make a nursemaid out of you, but that's the way it has to be. Being you're in the same berthing compartment as Martin, each and every morning, you check his rack and make sure he gets up. I've chewed Martin out, but that doesn't guarantee it won't happen again. I got Baker to stop this one. I can get Chief Madson to stop the next one. I may be able to get the next one stopped through the officers. From there, we've had it. I just thought you'd like to know that we now have strike one against us. We may not get four strikes as I've indicated."

Gray didn't appreciate his new roll, but knew it was necessary. He never said a word as he went back inside the Department Office, and I went back to my office.

When I walked in, Martin jumped to his feet. I knew I had been rough on him and had hurt his feelings. I didn't say a word. I sat down, and he sat down.

After a few minutes, I got up, and as I walked toward the door, I motioned for him to follow. Again we went up to Vultures Row. Just as we arrived, the last plane of this morning's flight OPS was maneuvering to get set on the catapult, ready for launch.

I reached into my pocket and pulled out a set of earplugs for each of us. After the last episode up here, I went to Sick Bay and picked up a couple of sets. As I showed them to him and handed him a set, the noise of the jet had vanished into the wild blue with the plane. He looked at the set, looked at the plane, and then looked at me.

He smiled a little then said, "Want to talk about it?"

"Yeah."

The rest of the cruise was uneventful and the ship was nearing the breakwater. Martin viewed the whole routine with a newfound excitement. He went from one viewing point to the next, not missing a thing, and he took me with him every step. It was almost as bad as trying to keep up with him and Janet at Disneyland. Maybe a repeat of the day we left port.

Before the ship finished tying up to the pier, we both spied Doris waiting for us.

On the way home, Jim explained every detail of the cruise and shrewdly omitted his getting put on report. Neither his enthusiasm nor his mouth ceased until after we had eaten.

Later in the evening after we settled down for some serious relaxing, Jim said, "Doris, I was put on report."

I was astonished he had brought it up and as far back as I can remember he had never called her "Doris." It had always been "Mrs. Wilson."

"I slept in one morning and the PPO put me on report. I know how you feel about the scheme, and I also know this jeopardized it. You have more at stake than I, so I thought you should know. I think it would be better if I told you rather than the Chief."

He related the whole incident as far as he knew. When he finished, Doris thanked him for being considerate, and she made no gesture of being upset.

Chapter 17

Thanksgiving morning Doris and I were knocking on the front door of the Martin residence. When Paul came to greet us, I said, "You're not going to cut me off this time are you Paul?"

He laughingly replied, "Not unless you have some notion of putting Dolly on that blooming boat."

"Ship, Paul. Ship!"

We laughed together, walked in, and gave our greetings to Dolly and Jim.

"Have a nice bus trip down last night, Jim?"

"Janet came down to the station to pick me up so that made it okay. I'm going over and pick her up in an hour or so. She's eating with us."

"Good," I replied and turned to Paul. "I've been here ten minutes, and no one has offered me a beer."

"You sailors are all alike. Just as soon as you hit a port, you've got to start drinking."

"No snide remarks, Paul. I want you to know that I have a file in my desk for blackmail purposes. Jim can verify that."

"Just give me a beer and quit blabbing naval secrets. Doris doesn't know these things of sailors and drinking."

"Believe me, I know," Doris replied. "But to keep from listening to any more of your 'naval secrets,' I'm going to let Dolly put me to work in the kitchen."

"I guess Jim has told you about his week at sea, hasn't he, Paul?"

"No, he hasn't. He came in quite late last night. I really expected him to come down with you. How about it, Jim? Tell me about the life of a swabbie and about the blackmail file. Am I missing something here?"

"Not now, Dad. Mr. Wilson heard my story at the end of the cruise when I told Mrs. Wilson. I'm sure he doesn't want to hear it again. Besides, I have to shower and dress. Got to pick up Janet, you know. Have Chief Wilson tell you. He can put more into it than I. I can assure you the Chief does have a blackmail file."

Paul looked at him and said, "So, it's 'Chief Wilson' and 'the Chief.' The words seem to flow quite smooth. No more 'Jack'?"

I came in with, "I just keep records. You know, kind of like people making phone calls when nobody is home after somebody just made the same phone call. You know, like two phone calls from San Diego."

Paul answered, "That's dirty, Jack."

"Most blackmail files are."

"I think I'm getting a message here that you have something on Dad. Is that right?"

"Son, don't you have an appointment? One that you need to attend . . . immediately?"

Jim left the room smiling, and after he was out of hearing distance, Paul continued.

"How is it really going, Jack? Is he giving you any trouble? You've got to be insane to keep up this fiasco."

"Paul, so far, it's exactly as I explained it to you in the beginning. There's not a hitch, no problems, and Jim is playing the role just perfect. Above all, there is no need to worry."

Paul listened as he went to the refrigerator to get beer.

I turned my head to the left and right, making sure Jim was not within hearing distance, I asked Paul if he knew of the relation that existed between Jim and Janet. He said he knew they were extremely thick and he expected it to get thicker.

"Well, it is just about as thick as it can get right now."

"It's all right with me. Jim can take care of himself and make his own decisions, as you're well aware. I want him to get a good job if he expects to support two people. Remember, I'm the one that wants him to go to college."

"Don't get me wrong, Paul. I think it's great. I think Janet is a nice young lady, and as far as I know, she seems right for him."

"How do you know so much about them, and especially her?"

I told him of Janet's spending the night a while back and that Jim and I have had some quite intimate talks.

"I imagine there are times when it is easier for him to talk to me than it is his own father," I said.

"As I say, Dolly and I have expected such, so it isn't as much as a secret as they would care to think it is," he replied. "So much for that stuff. I want to hear the details of 'Sailor Jim.'"

"If I'm going to tell the story, or even the part I know, let's go into the kitchen and sit at the table. I don't want to go through it twice. Of course, Doris has her story. You may want to hear some of her side also."

As we sat down, Paul propped his elbows on the table with his hands under his chin as would be expected of a child listening to a bedtime story. I stopped dead still and looked at him. He looked back at me said, "So?"

I replied, "Your listening position. It isn't that interesting?" I paused. We both laughed.

"Well Paul, I can't really say much more than I already have. There are times when he seems to be over polite to some people and of course, over friendly toward me. He's really doing a fine job in my office."

"Now that's the stuff I want to know," Paul interrupted. "I didn't know exactly where he was working. Exactly what does he do? Is he learning anything?"

"Okay. He works in my office, for me, and he does general office work such as typing, filing, running errands, keeping records of the technical publications, probably TOs to you, and he keeps the office clean. He logs the division training in individual training folders and keeps inventories of the divisions equipment. As far as work goes, there is no manual labor, but the job he does is necessary, and he does it well."

I noticed Paul was about to speak so I said, "That's right, it's a dirty job, but someone has to do it."

We both laughed.

"At the present, his two closest friends are the two collaborators of mine."

"About these two characters? Are they typical sailors or are they pretty good guys?" Paul asked.

"I sure resent that question," I retorted. "Typical sailors or pretty good guys? Wouldn't care to rephrase that would you, Paul?"

"All right," he said. "He isn't being lead astray, is he?"

"You're doing just fine. Just keep digging the grave. The only place he goes with them is to chow. At night, he's with me except for this past week at sea. Get me another beer." This I said as though it were one sentence for I had finished the first beer and needed an interruption in the conversation.

I got an interruption. Not the one I expected or wanted to hear.

It was Doris. "Jack, I talked to Frances Swanson this week. It seems as though some more of the doctor patient confidentiality has leaked. You never told me you went back. Want me to continue?"

Paul asked, "What does this mean? What has that got to do with the story?"

"The doctor she's speaking of is the doctor aboard ship who says I have ulcer problems. He is Frances' husband. Frances is in the LPGA with Doris."

"Okay, so you have ulcers, drink as you like cause there's no skin off my nose. Continue telling us of Jim's week at sea," Paul said as he walked toward the refrigerator.

"Just about the only thing I can say is that he was quite excited. As each new interest or experience arose, he gave it his full attention. He was like a kid with a new toy. Sometimes as I'm watching him I think he would make a good actor. He's doing a good job of it now.

"As far as the way he feels and or thinks, I think it would be better if he told you, but I don't think he will. How can I describe his emotions?

"I take that back. There is one thing I can tell you.

"Our office is directly under the flight deck and when the first plane landed, Jim liked to have came unglued. He almost jumped out of his skin. I thought I was going to have to scrape him off the overhead. Then he looked at me. It was one of those looks that you have when you look to see if anyone was looking at you. Kind of an 'I'm embarrassed, sure hope no one was watching' looks.

"It's quite a thing to have an airplane crash just feet above your head.

"Also, while I'm thinking about it. I'd like to suggest that you get Jim a good camera for Christmas. Look at me Paul. Read my lips. A good camera! I repeat, 'A good camera.' I'm sure he'll give it a good workout on the cruise.

"Changing the subject again. I want to bring up the cruise. When I say, 'The Cruise,' I'm speaking of the overseas tour. We have a one-week cruise starting Monday and then on the 28th of December, we head west. You might bring this up when Jim and Janet get back. We'll be gone from 28 December till 5 July. Just a little over six months. That is provided everything goes right."

"What do you mean provided everything goes right?"

"Paul, I don't control world politics. We're heading straight to Vietnam. You know that's getting to be one big mess over there.

"Who knows what all could possibly happen. If anything does happen, he'll be there for the duration. Whatever that means."

We talked for about an hour and a half, and I was the one talking as Jim walked in with Janet. She was dressed very nicely and the beauty of her youth radiated as she entered. She was a show stealer. I had definitely been upstaged.

We all talked for a brief period, and shortly thereafter I whispered to Jim that we talked about his week at sea, but I hadn't mentioned the report incident. Again, if it were to be brought up, it would be up to him. Frankly, I didn't believe it was any of their business.

The weather was beautiful so Paul, Jim, and I continued our talks on the patio.

Meal preparations progressed smoothly, and Janet assisted rather than act as a guest. The apron she wore just didn't fit in with such a young and beautiful woman in such a beautiful dress. Surely this was not the same young girl who went to Disneyland with us, the schoolgirl in jeans.

Time passed rapidly, and we were soon seated, eating turkey, and still discussing "Sailor Jim." Jim was questioned, teased, and remained the topic of the conversation throughout the meal.

Paul hinted of Jim and Janet's engagement. Janet commented just enough to let it be known that marriage plans were in the air and no more.

The meal was delicious, and soon it was time for Doris and I to go.

"Well, Dolly, I want to thank you for the wonderful meal and a nice day. It was truly just wonderful," I said sincerely. "Jim, as you know, we're supposed to report in for muster either Saturday or Sunday. We can't take more than 72 hours off, so I'll tell you what I'm going to do. I have the duty Saturday so I will muster you in. That way, you can have the rest of the weekend off. Of course, don't blab this back aboard the ship.

"Catch the bus back Sunday evening, and I'll come down and pick you up at the station. You can spend the night with us."

It was starting to get dark, so we said our good-byes and headed the Buick north.

Chapter 18

Everything took a normal course for the next month. Jim learned more about his job, more about the ship, and more about the Navy.

Christmas had passed three days ago. Jim went to San Diego while Doris and I spent some quiet time together. It was time for us to leave on our WestPac cruise.

The ship was to get underway at 1000. This gave us plenty of time to say good-bye to our families. Paul, Dolly, and Janet drove up from San Diego and arrived at our house near 0630. Jim and I went to the ship at 0715. The rest said they would be on the pier at 0830. This gave us time to muster and store the belongings that we packed at the last minute. This also gave the others a chance to rest a bit from their drive.

At 0815, I met Jim at the afterbrow. He had his dress uniform on and carried a camera. He said it was his Christmas present from his parents.

Shortly after we met, he took pictures of the crowd of people on the pier who came to say bon voyage to the ship and crew. A few minutes passed then we saw our group walking toward the ship.

Jim took more pictures.

After they boarded, we strolled from hangar bay to hangar bay. We talked while trying to find a place where we could have a little privacy.

A pact was made between Jim and I that we would meet with he and Janet in the Avionics Office in thirty minutes. This would give him a few minutes to be alone with Janet while Paul, Dolly, Doris, and I went below to the Chiefs' Mess for a cup of coffee.

While having our coffee, I reassured Paul and Dolly that Jim would be perfectly safe and that he would return in the same condition in which he left except that he would have a little more worldly knowledge.

We arrived in the Avionics Office and found Jim and Janet were already there. They had been up on the flight deck, taken a few pictures, and had gone to the office to have absolute privacy for a few minutes before we came in. Jim briefly explained his job, and all too soon we heard over the 1MC, "Now hear this. Now hear this. All visitors are requested to leave the ship."

We locked the office and walked down the ladder toward the after brow.

Janet was no longer trying to hide the tears that rolled down her cheeks. Paul's voice reflected his sadness and Dolly could no longer hide her tears. Doris and I followed suit.

I've said good-bye many, many times, and each time it becomes more difficult. It seems to be such an unnecessary thing. After I have said good-bye like this, I am completely fatigued. This time was no exception. I realized too soon I was leaving that which I loved most . . . my wife.

Paul and I shook hands. Dolly gave me a hug and a kiss. Doris and I kissed and embraced each other quite tightly. Jim received the same from Janet. This was to be our last moment together for a long time.

Again the 1MC blared that same ruthless quotation, "All visitors and guests are requested to leave the ship." One more time, as we neared the afterbrow, the 1MC quote changed a bit, "All visitors and guests are requested to depart the ship at this time."

I thought, "How cold . . ."

Soon all the guests were off and the afterbrow was removed from the ship.

Our guests remained on the pier waving their hands and watching.

All lines were cast off and we were underway. The ship slowly backed out and away from the pier. The Martins, Janet, and Doris could still be seen on the pier. Again I thought, "What a waste. I hate leaving her. I swore never again . . . never again."

As we moved farther and farther out, the people on the pier became an unidentifiable crowd.

Jim had taken his pictures and I was exhausted. I also wanted to be alone so I retired to the Chief's Quarters.

As Jim and I departed, I told him I would be in the office later in the day, and once more I told myself, "Never, never again."

Chapter 19

When Jim came into the office, I could see the excitement in his eyes. They were telling me he had been at sea for five days and now there was land out there. Not just any land, but Hawaii. I could see the first thrill of setting foot upon a distant land.

He couldn't hide the sparkle, though he tried. He walked over to me and said, "What are you going to do today, Chief?"

"Nothing in particular. Why?"

"I thought maybe you would show Hawaii to me."

"You don't think I'm going to play tourist while you are the tourist and take your picture do you?" I questioned and accentuated the "you" and "your."

In a disappointed tone, he answered, "I was hoping you would."

"Of course I will Jim. I just couldn't pass the opportunity to try to burst your excitement-inflated balloon. As a matter of fact, I have mentally mapped out a plan of attack. I was hoping you would ask me to tag along with you."

"Don't get too carried away. I've promised Gray and Whitteker I would go out with them."

"I've anticipated such. Go with me tonight and tomorrow. During this time I'll show you all that you'll want pictures of and from then on, the rest of your time will be just that. Yours."

"Fine. What do you have on the hook?"

"I planned to show you downtown Honolulu this afternoon, and from there we will go to Waikiki. For tomorrow, I thought of taking the bus tour offered by Special Services."

"Sounds great to me. Gray and Whitteker have tour tickets for tomorrow. Do you?"

"I have them right here," I answered and fished in my pocket. I pulled out the two tickets for proof. "Now the important thing is, do you have enough film? I'd sure hate for that new camera to sit idle."

"No chance of that. Yes, I do have film and again, I want to thank you for the flash attachment you gave me as a Christmas present. The whole outfit is just super. Thanks."

"Your Dad and I got together on that. You can thank him. Let's go out and take a look at Hawaii. One more thing, don't you dare tell anyone here on the ship I gave that present to you."

We had just passed Diamond Head and were just about parallel with Honolulu. It wouldn't be long now before we tied up at one of the fuel piers at the Supply Depot.

Jim and I went up to the flight deck, and as we crossed over to the starboard side of the ship, I asked, "Jim, do you have any regrets about coming on the trip? That's not exactly how I want to phrase it. Do you feel out of place? That didn't seem to come out right either. How do you feel about the scheme now?"

"I don't feel out of place as much now as I did the first week. I feel more like I'm part of the crew. I know just about everyone in the division and quite a few of the other guys in the department. I've made speaking type of acquaintances with a few others. There's one guy that makes me feel uneasy. He's a friend of Whitteker's and works in disbursing. We have chow together every once in a while. Other than little things like that, all's fine. Oh yes, I still don't have much use for our friendly PPO."

I laughed out loud at that for I thought maybe Jim had earned the right to dislike him.

We walked back to the port side of the ship as we passed the USS Arizona. Attention was piped over the 1MC system and was followed by, "Attention to port."

We stood erect and saluted, and we passed by the memorial. We finished our salute, and I know Jim had an uneasy feeling within as he looked at me.

"What do you know about the Arizona?" he asked.

"Not much and I don't want to talk about it."

There was no need for him to know that my only two uncles were still aboard and that was one of the influencing factors concerning my joining the Navy.

After that, we watched more scenery pass and went back to the office.

When liberty call sounded I told Jim that he could go get ready to go on liberty. "There's no need to rush. There are too many men trying to get off at the same time. I just can't see fighting the mob. We'll meet at the afterbrow in two hours. This will give both of us plenty of time. See you then."

With that, we locked the office and went our separate ways.

Chief Petty Officers are authorized to have civilian clothes on board. I'd thought of wearing my civvies but rather than have Jim feel uneasy, I wore my tropical white long uniform which consisted of a white cap cover, a short sleeve shirt, long trousers, and white shoes.

Jim was at the afterbrow waiting when I arrived. I took less than an hour to get ready, and I was sure I'd be some time ahead of him. He got dressed so fast I am not sure he got wet in the shower. He did rush it. When I approached him I could see his excitement. He was definitely ready to go.

We walked off the ship and down the pier. When we came to the end, we hailed a taxi to the Base Exchange. We reached our destination, and the fare was ninety cents. I thought the fare was high, and when I paid the man, I turned to Jim and said, "Welcome to Hawaii." This was to insinuate the fare was high, and I wanted to make sure the driver heard me. Prices in Hawaii have always been out of this world.

We shopped in the exchange, and it was then Jim began to understand. When he would pick up a piece of woodcarving and look at the price, his eyes would bug out and again I would whisper, "Welcome to Hawaii."

Being he would have a later chance to buy souvenirs, I advised him to buy light or minor items to keep from having to carry them all over town.

We bought nothing for we mutually agreed to leave now and return later for a shopping spree.

Our next leg of this excursion was downtown Honolulu so we walked out the main gate and over to the bus stop. The taxi transportation fee was ninety cents for just over one half a mile and the bus was twenty-five cents for about six miles. We boarded and were soon on our way.

"This is it. Beautiful downtown Honolulu," I said as we stepped off the bus.

He replied, "Looks like any other city to me . . . like downtown San Diego."

"I have a couple of things to show you, and then we will be on our way again."

We walked down to the Aloha Tower, to the statue of King Kamehameha, and a couple of other standard tourist attractions. Jim took pictures of the sights and I took pictures of Jim as he stood alongside the points of interest. He looked at a very large Monkey Pod tree.

When he satisfied himself he had enough pictures, we caught the next bus to Waikiki.

Our bus stopped in front of the International Market Place. I decided this was just about the best place to start. As we strolled through the open-air shops, I noticed there had been many changes since I last passed through.

The first change hit me as I stepped off the bus. "Don the Beachcomber" was no longer there. It had been replaced by what I call a "diddy bopper" type place with loud "acid" music. I tried to ignore the loud music as it came out of the door and from the sidewalk speakers. It was totally impossible.

Most of the other changes were of a remodeling nature and as these appeared to be unimpressive, I watched Jim.

Jim just didn't have enough eyes to take in all he was seeing. I know he was trying to mentally pick gifts for his parents and Janet. While trying to pick gifts, he was weighing each item against the contents of his billfold. He would pick up an item, scrutinize it, look at the price, shake his head, and set it back down.

As we browsed through the loop of the place, I explained how it was the last time I visited.

Jim bought a comic newspaper that stated on the headlines he got married at Waikiki Beach. He also purchased an envelope with it and mailed the paper back to Janet.

I told him he was going to get killed for that.

We completed the loop and headed for the beach. Everyone has to see Waikiki Beach. As it has been every time I'd been there, the place was a big nothing. The water was dead and the people present, near the same. Two types of people lounge on the beach. Hippies, or that type of person, who have nothing to do or contribute to the world and the rest are tourist of the upper portion of the middle class who have come to Hawaii for their once-in-a-life-time vacation. Then they go back to East Cupcake where they tell their friends and neighbors about how wonder-ful of a place it is and how they enjoyed it. Maybe they do enjoy it. I don't.

I sensed Jim's disappointment so we continued our window-shopping along the streets. When he decided he had seen enough, we agreed to get a bite to eat and end the evening with the movie "Dr. Zhivago."

Chapter 20

It was hardly after 0900 when Dave LaRue came into the Avionics Office. I hadn't seen him in close to six years.

"Well, I'll be," was my opening statement to my guest and my friend of over fourteen years. "What in the world are you doing aboard this thing?"

"Search and destroy. I was told to search out your young duff and kick it a few times."

He walked in and over to my desk. I stood and we shook hands. As we held each other at arms length, I scrutinized his uniform. "And I might ask, what in the world are you doing in a Chief's uniform?"

"Just yesterday I found this pudgy Chief drunk in an alley so I stole it. I left his naked body lying right where I found it."

"Well Dave, you're looking good. Really, when did you make Chief?"

"Yesterday. I went through the initiation ceremonies at Lemoore just after lunch. Finished up my paperwork and caught a flight out of Lemoore to Travis Air Force Base then landed in Honolulu about eleven last night. Sneaked aboard, found a bunk, and crashed near 0100 this morning."

"I didn't see you at chow. How did you know I was aboard?"

"I got up late. The cook prepared me a special breakfast of eggs and hash browns. When I finished, I asked who ran the Avionics Shop. When I was told 'Jack Wilson,' I said, 'horse manure,' and here I am."

"Dave, excuse my manners. I would like to introduce Lieutenant Carter, my division officer, Jim Martin, my coolie, and Bob Yancey, our calibration technician.

"This rascal is Dave LaRue. He and I were stationed together a couple of times and we've known each other since AT "A" school when were a couple of young punk kids. You're looking good Dave. Real good."

"You're looking pretty good with that star in your collar device yourself. When did you get that?"

"Just the other day I found this pudgy E-8 drunk in an alley so I took his collar devices. It must have been just before you got to him."

"Jack, you're still as full of bologna as you ever were. I'm surprised Doris never got around to kicking some of it out of you. I knew long ago she should have slapped you around a few times with one of her golf clubs.

"You are still married to her aren't you?"

"Sure am. She couldn't chase me off . . . even with one of her golf clubs. Did you ever get married?"

"Sure did. You remember when we left NAS Jax? Well, I went to a VX outfit down at Boca Chica. Met this sweet young thing and got married. It was fine until I got orders for recruiting duty in Traverse City, Michigan. That was when I really found out I married a Florida girl. There was no way she was going up there. She just never did like this fat boy."

"And you talk about me being full of it. Dave, I've never been able to hold a candle to you. Let's get out of here and get down to some serious lying. You haven't told the truth since you walked through the door."

Dave acknowledged the acquaintance of our office personnel, and we went below to the Chiefs' Mess.

Over a few cups of coffee, we continued our one upmanship on each other and even sprinkled the truth in every so often just to bring each other up to date.

He explained that he was with the VA Detachment for the cruise and would be assigned to the ship's Avionics Shop.

"Now just what in the meantime am I supposed to do with you in my shop? I already have one E-7 sleeping in there."

"That's the only reason they sent me aboard. I'm supposed to keep an eye on the other men that we've sent up to your shop, and I'm supposed to oversee our APG radar. Other than that, I'm yours baby."

"Seriously, I don't need you. Chief Hawkins, the E-7 I spoke of, does a fine job. He runs the shop. I run the office. However, if your CO wants you to hang around, muster with us, and keep an eye on his gear, that's fine. You'll probably wind up doing less than I do."

"Fine. Now that we have that settled, let's get off here and get down to some serious drinking. I hardly had a chance to get my fair share at the initiation yesterday."

"Can't Dave. Got a couple of problems. The kid you met in my office, Jim Martin? I promised him I'd go on a tour of the island with him today. Second, I have a little stomach problem."

"Jack, are you saying you got ulcers? I've had 'em. Didn't like it much. Drown the rascals. The kid can take care of himself. Who wiped our noses back in Memphis?"

"I'll tell you what I'll do. I'll go with the kid this afternoon and meet you at the EM Club later this evening. How does that sound? We have about six months in front of us to get down to serious drinking."

We concluded this would be the plan of attack for the day. I'd go with the kid for the afternoon; he'd get his gear properly stored, and later sneak a snooze.

It seemed to be an easy plan, and it went well until near noon. I left Whitteker, Gray, and Martin at the end of the tour so they could do their thing, whatever that was, without being chaperoned.

I went back to the ship, caught a couple of Z's on my own, and toyed with my evening chow. After that I took a couple of my antacid tablets and grabbed a cab to meet Dave, wishing I hadn't made the promise.

It must have been around 10:30 when the three young sailors came into the club and came over to where Dave and I were sitting in a booth. I had downed enough beers to where I didn't give a hoot about my ulcers. I could always take care of them tomorrow.

Whitteker, Gray, and Martin were all about three sheets to the wind. We tried to ignore them to the best of our abilities, and yet I tried hinting to Gray to get Martin back the aboard ship.

Among their slurs, some real and some put on, I heard mentioned about their quickly leaving some other bar. I let it completely pass.

Dave and I were trying to talk and swap more sea stories. In the midst of Dave's talking, he again mentioned not getting his fair share of the beer at the initiation yesterday.

That's when it happened!

Martin said, "You want your fair share of the beer and an initiation? Here!"

He picked up a pitcher of beer and poured it over Chief LaRue's head.

The beer went all over the table and some into my lap. Dave yelled a string of cuss words as he jumped up and took a swing at Martin.

Whitteker had his back to the table when the action started and turned around to see the commotion. As he did, he turned into the path of Dave's swing and caught it on the shoulder.

I grabbed Gray and yelled, "Get Martin out of here right now!"

Whitteker made a lunge for Dave. Dave made a lunge for Martin. Gray grabbed Martin first, and they made a quick exit.

I got in between Chief LaRue and Whitteker before any damage was done to either.

The whole incident seemed to take only a few seconds. Before I could really do or say anything, two other sailors grabbed Whitteker and assisted in his forced exit.

"Dave, I'm sorry. I had no idea."

"I think I'll kill him. Where did you get him? Yes, I'm going to kill him."

"Maybe you won't get a chance. I'll see him first and maybe I'll kill him. Want to flip a coin to see who gets the first crack at a contract on the kid?"

"Jack. I'm serious. Just look at this uniform. Not only was it clean, it was brand new. This is the first time I ever put on."

"Well, look at mine."

He answered, "Ain't nothing wrong except that it looks like you wet your britches."

That was when I looked him over good and snickered. When I laughed, he started to laugh.

We laughed out loud together, and he said, "You remember that one night . . ."

I cut him short and said, "In Jax."

We both knew what incident we were thinking of and laughing about. We walked out of the club together laughing with and at each other.

Chapter 21

When in port, some things for some people are quite lax. I slept in. I didn't make it up to the office until after nine. When I arrived, I stayed in the passageway just outside the office. I slightly cracked the door, saw Martin, and I motioned with my finger for him to come outside.

Once more I tried to be calm, cool, and collected about last night's incident.

Martin followed as we climbed our way upon to the flight deck. As we strolled toward the bow, I said, "It's crazy stunts like you pulled light night that gets a lot of people into a lot of trouble. Personal feelings get hurt. Physical damage occurs. Legal problems arise. What you did last night was a basic insult to me, to a personal friend of mine of many years, and to be just as honest as I can, I was humiliated. I was ashamed of you and of myself for having brought you on board to place you into a position of such embarrassment. I want, I insist, and I demand that you apologize to Chief LaRue in your most humble manner.

"You see, Jim, the Navy is not just a job. It's a life. Many of the people you meet and work with today will be transferred and never seen or heard of again. On the other hand, many will circulate and will show up on you doorstep many years later. These are the ones that you want to be your friends. At the first crossing of paths of strangers, you don't know who will or will not be back around. This is why you have to seek out those you would like to be your friends and treat them with respect and with dignity.

"Dave LaRue and I were about your age when we met. We seemed to hit it off together from the start. Since that time, we have been stationed together on both sides of these United States, and we've carried our friendship with us in our absence. We've yelled at each other. We've been drunk together many times. Later, maybe at the next duty station, we would get cross-threaded with each other, then the next thing you know we were back together as close friends. This is why I was happy to see him. He, as so many others in the Navy, is like a family to me. It's extremely difficult to explain. Maybe you don't understand what I'm trying to tell you, but basically, it's a way of life. You'll learn this as you grow older.

"This is me, this is my life. This is why I emphatically demand that you speak with Chief LaRue."

We continued to walk.

"Chief, I woke up last night when the compartment was spinning. I barely made it to the head. As I was hugging the commode and relieving my stomach I first thought of how miserable I felt. As I propped myself up against the bulkhead and became more and more sober, I began to think of you. I thought of how I embarrassed you in front of your friends, and that was when I became more ashamed of myself.

"I never went back to my rack. I cleaned myself up and started walking throughout the ship. I sat on one of the sponsons and watched the lights on shore. As I watched the sunrise, I had already made up my mind to find Chief LaRue and apologize. I found him near an A4 on the hanger deck.

"When I finished my prepared speech he just looked at me. Sort of strange like it was. Finally he walked off. He never said a word. He just walked off."

Martin and I walked together for a few minutes without speaking.

Martin broke the silence with, "Do you think he's setting me up for the kill?"

I stopped and said, "I don't know."

With that, I motioned with my thumb and pointed back toward the fantail of the ship indicating for him to return to the office.

I continued my walk. It was then I became aware that not only am I and Chief LaRue alike in oh so many ways, Jim Martin appears to fit the same mold. Just younger, that's all, just younger.

Chapter 22

I was still wandering around the flight deck thinking of the talk that I had just had when I heard a familiar voice shouting from behind me.

"Hey, Chief! Chief Wilson, wait up."

It was Gray. He was running up the flight deck to catch up with me.

As he approached, almost out of breath, he said, "Chief, we've been looking for you and calling all over the place. I just now ran into Martin and he said you were up here. Well, anyhow, Baker wants to see you. He's told everyone that he has to talk to you. He says it's very important and has asked me to help find you."

"What seems to be his problem?"

"He seemed to be bent out of shape. I couldn't it make out. He wouldn't say why he needed to talk to you, he just said it was very important."

"Where's he at now?"

"He thought maybe the best way to find you was for him to stay put so he's waiting at the entrance to the Chiefs' Mess."

"Thanks, I'll find him."

Well, find him I did. That was the beginning of the whole mess.

He said, "Chief, I've got to talk to you. It's urgent and definitely has to be private. Follow me."

I had no idea where we were going, but I followed. We closed the door behind us as we went into the chain locker on the forecastle. There was only he and I and of course, the anchor chain.

"Chief, I got into a lot of trouble last night. It all started innocent as they always do. I was minding my own business and having a nice quiet beer by myself.

"Well, it wasn't quiet. The stereo in the place was blaring and a go-go girl was dancing. I didn't pay much attention to her, well, to anybody cause I was thinking about Linda and Janie . . . my wife and daughter. Anyhow, this guy next to me keeps bugging me. I tried to ignore him, but he kept it up. He was picking on anything and everything trying to get under my skin. When I had just about all I could take, instead of leaving, I hit the bastard.

"Normally, I don't do things like that. But a guy can only take so much.

"It wound up being quite a fight. It was fast and furious, and we busted the place up a bit. You know, a couple of chairs, a table or two, some pitchers of beer and of course, glasses. When the Shore Patrol came in, the other guy was on the deck, and I was stabbing at him with the legs of a barstool.

"I'm not saying it wasn't my fault. I know I should have left the joint. But I didn't. Before I knew it, the place was full of Honolulu Police, Hawaiian Armed Service Police and Shore Patrol. I was cuffed and taken to the Police Station. I was put through the whole nine yards and brought back to the ship this morning and turned over to the Master at Arms.

"I was roughed up by the police and such, but I kept telling myself, 'You deserve it you jerk.' You know I try to do my job well and like I said, I don't normally do things like that.

"This morning in the MAA shack, those who I thought were my friends, treated me as if they never knew me. Their whole attitude changed. I had become a common criminal. Anyhow, they now have me on quite a list of charges. Now, I want you to get me out of it. I can't afford a bust. Linda and Janie are having a rough time as it is.

"You've got to help me, Chief. You owe me, and you're the only one I can turn to."

I bought the whole story. I kept my cool and listened as he did all the talking, but when he said you owe me, it rubbed me wrong.

"Wait just a minute! Maybe I do owe you as you put it, but I think that would be more in terms of inter departmental type stuff. You're in a sling with the big guys. That's a little out of my jurisdiction."

"Chief, I need your help. I'm not just asking for you help, I'm pleading. I know this is serious stuff, but I didn't think it would go this far."

I pushed my cap back over the crown of my head, stuck my finger in my ear, and scratched a bit as I tried to think.

My feelings sank.

I thought some more and finally said, "Okay Baker. I'll see what I can do."

He immediately replied, "That's not good enough, Chief. You've got to get me out of this mess."

"For crying out loud, I can't make any promises! I can only try. I'll talk to Chief Madson first and see what he thinks or see if he can do anything."

He wasn't satisfied or even close to happy over my decision. He had hardly calmed down.

I first went by the MAA shack and found out what were the charges. They had him and they were playing it for what it was worth.

When I left there, I felt a little bit like Baker. I didn't like their attitude. Anyone would have thought they caught John Dillinger or maybe Al Capone.

Nevertheless, I was going to give it a try. Chief Madson, our Leading Chief was next.

It was during lunch I found him in the Chiefs' Mess.

"What ya up to, Jack?" he asked as he continued eating.

"Just found out the mess the PPO is in. What do you know about it?"

"Haven't given it much thought. The dumb cluck got into a fight. Master at Arms called me this morning. Went up there to see what it was about. That's about it. He has gotten himself into a big mess. What's it to you? How did you get into it?"

"Well, it looks as if I've got another one."

"Meaning?"

"You once said Martin looked up to me like I was his daddy. Baker has come to me and asked me to get him off."

Madson said, "You asked for it. You good old boys seem to attract 'em like . . ." He paused then said, "I won't say it while we're eating."

I asked, "Well?"

"Well what?"

"I'm asking if you think we can get him off?"

"What's this we stuff? Got a mouse in your pocket?"

"No. I mean we . . . like you and I. Know what I mean? The kid came to me, and I'm coming to you. The guy is a good worker and he does his job well. Ever had any trouble from him before?"

"No. He is a good worker, and he does his job well, but he asked for it. He knows better than to get into a bind like that."

"No. We can't let it end there. You going to help?"

"Nope."

"Thanks loads, Chief. It's really appreciated," I said sarcastically.

He finished eating and leaned back in his chair as I ate. He kept watching me. I could feel his eyes.

After I finished I said, "I want you to know, I'm not going to stop. I'm going to see Lieutenant Carter and then I'm going to the Commander. I've seen the list of charges they have against him, and I've noted the attitude of the MAA's. I thought the charges were picky-picky, and he's asked for my help. The combinations say I've got to try."

"Don't stir the pot, Jack."

"Is that an order or a request?"

"It's a request." He paused again but didn't take his eyes off me. "Okay. You talk to Lieutenant Carter and I'll see the Commander. How's that?"

I never replied as he got up from his chair and left the mess.

I smiled a bit to myself.

I talked with Lieutenant Carter that afternoon, and he just flowed with the tide. Easiest going son of a gun I ever met. He said he'd talk with the Commander.

I never saw the Leading Chief until the evening meal. I picked him out again and sat at his table.

"Jack, can't I eat in peace?"

I gave it back to him. "Nope."

"I talked with the Commander, Lieutenant Carter talked to him then he called me back in. We talked with the Master at Arms and all the picky-picky stuff, as you call it, has been dropped. They still have him on disorderly conduct and destruction of private property. How's that?"

"That's all right. Now we have only two more charges to go." I grinned.

"Drop it, Jack!"

I answered back, "Order or request?"

"Request. I quit." He left me by myself once again.

I couldn't let it go at that. I had to try another approach so the next morning I went to the Legal Office and spoke with the legal officer, Ltjg. Harcourt.

Normally I have no trouble talking with people. This guy was very difficult. He was cold to anything I said. He informed me it was none of my business and to butt out. He said it was his job to prosecute and to suggest to the Executive Officer what he deemed appropriate punishment.

I left his office quite disgruntled after he said he was going to recommend that Baker be busted at least one stripe, pay for all the damages and that he be restricted to the ship for the duration of the cruise.

I went to the Chiefs' Mess to cool off. I didn't want to be around anyone.

The next morning I was calmed somewhat. I was sitting in my office when Martin came in. He sensed I wasn't my usual self.

"Hey, Chief, want to go to the beach and buy some souvenirs?" he asked.

I replied, "Not really. I have some business to attend today. Why don't you go by yourself and pick out what you want?" I gave him $200. "You think that will be enough to buy something for Janet, your mother, and father? And, of course, yourself." I continued, "We're getting underway tomorrow. Stay out of the beer joints."

While we are in port like this, shop work seems to be at a minimum. Liberty is of prime importance to the crew, but we get accomplished all that is required with just a skeleton crew.

I touched base with my Shop Chief, and Chief LaRue was getting his men and equipment lined out. Everything seemed to be smooth.

I went back to my cubbyhole and really wasn't surprised to see the PPO waiting.

"I've talked with the Master at Arms and they told me it was out of their hands. Everything was turned over to the legal office."

I replied, "Yeah, I know. The legal officer and I had a talk. Short, but it was a talk. He wants you to pay for the damages in the bar. That is, on top of the bust and restriction that he's going to suggest to the XO."

"Can't do it, Chief. I can't afford a bust and I can't afford to pay any damages. You've got to get me out of this mess completely."

"For crying out loud, Baker . . . I can only do so much. I've tried. The Leading Chief has tried and so have Lieutenant Carter and the Maintenance Officer. If that Commander can't do much, how do you expect me to do more?"

"They don't have a personal interest, Chief. To them, I'm just a number . . . one of the crew. Know what I mean?"

"I know what you mean. Still, there's only so much a person can do before it's completely out of his realm. Know what I mean?"

He answered, "I've found out that the XO isn't going to be with us when we leave Hawaii. He's flown back to the States, and the mast won't be until after he gets back. The old man is taking us through ORI. He'll have his hands full with that and any rinky dink stuff is put off. We still have about two weeks. I ask that you keep trying."

Our Operational Readiness Inspection is our last exercises before going to Southeast Asia. We were finishing last minute loading and preparations. Tomorrow would start seventy-two hours of extensive maneuvers.

Baker left my office, and the more I sat and thought about that legal officer, the more upset I became.

Doc Swanson told me I could ease off his liquid chalk, and he prescribed Zantac. I took one hoping it would ease my stomach. I also took some headache pills. I must be a nervous wreck. Why can't people leave me alone? Drinking seems to be the only thing that gets someone through messes like this and now I couldn't even do that. Well, not very well now.

I had enough. I went back to see the legal officer.

We sat in his office and got right to the point.

Now you talk about a short fuse, Ltjg. Harcourt really had one. He practically kicked me out of his office. As the old saying goes, "I've been kicked out of lot better places than that." That didn't bother me too much, but when he started picking on Chiefs that ruffled my feathers.

"You Chiefs think you run this Navy. Well, let me tell you, you don't! It's the officers like myself with college educations that run this Navy. All you guys do is sit around and expect everybody else do your work. I do my own work. I'm the one who says who will be prosecuted and who won't."

"Wait just a minute, Lieutenant! It's you who doesn't understand the Navy. You're not up for re-election. You're career doesn't depend on how many cases you bring to court and how many you win. This is the Navy not some stupid political game. This is about people, about men, about who is going to stick around and see that our mission is accomplished. This is never going to happen with people like you and your attitude!"

He came right back, "Chief, you talk to me like that and I'll have you up on insubordination charges faster than you could believe possible. Now get out! I don't ever want to see you back in this office again."

When I left his office, I was so angry I could have bit a nail in two.

I went to the Chiefs' Mess and got a cup of coffee. It wasn't what I wanted. I called the shop and got hold of Chief LaRue. He met me in the mess.

He walked in, pitched his hat on one of the empty chairs between us. "What happened, old buddy? You seemed quite urgent."

"I want a drink. I know you've got a few bottles stashed in your locker."

We went to the berthing compartment and broke out a bottle. Over a few sneaky drinks I told him my story. He became upset over Harcourt's attitude.

We went back to the mess and got a cup of coffee. I took a shot of Doc Swanson's cure all while we were in the berthing compartment.

I still hadn't relaxed when Chief Madson joined us. He said as he sat down, "What are you two grouches up to? Lose your last friend? Eat, drink, and be merry." He paused then said, "Speaking of drinking, you two stink to high heavens."

Chief LaRue said, "It's Lieutenant Harcourt. Your legal officer. He's got Jack bent out of shape, and I didn't care for what he said about Chiefs. He had better watch his tongue or he'll be taking a midnight swim."

"He must have said something to get the both of you rattled. Let's have the whole thing."

Once again I related my story.

Chief Madson said, "Listen Jack. I tried to get you to stay out of it. But no, you had to keep it up. Just let the Lieutenant be. Let him live in his fancy little officer world and you keep out of it. I'll talk with him and settle the waves you're causing. It's best we nip this in the bud and get back on an even keel. There's no need to start a long cruise with this attitude." He stood up then said, "Jack, you keep your nose out of it. If you don't, you'll have to answer to me. And believe me, you don't want that to happen. I'll make you the most miserable Chief in the Pacific. Do you read me, Jack? Jack! Look at me when I'm talking to you! Do you understand me?"

I answered, "Yeah."

"I mean it, Jack. I'm not going to mess around with you, and I mean it! That goes for you too, LaRue. I'm not putting up with this."

He left Dave and I. We got ourselves another cup of coffee and were doing more looking at it than drinking. We seldom spoke.

Finally he said, "You know, Jack? You and I can get into trouble without half trying. Remember in Oceana when you and I got drunk and turned that skunk loose in the Chief's barracks around three in the morning? Now that raised a stink."

We were starting to get in a better mood.

It couldn't have been thirty minutes before Chief Madson came back in. We were still at the same table.

He was worse than when he left as he said, "You've done it, Jack. That Jg. jumped the Personnel Chief after you left and got him bent clear out of shape. That Lieutenant started in on me with the Chief stuff. I told him he'd better go back and read some naval history. Well, the next thing you know he lit my fire. I told him he didn't know what he was talking about or who he was talking to. Jack, from now on . . . I want you to remember you started this mess."

Once again he left us. I hadn't said a word to him, but I could tell that Lieutenant got him started.

I said to Dave, "I guess we better go back to sitting on our duff. ORI is a waiting." The rest of the day was smooth even though I remained disgruntled.

Martin came back with some nice gifts. I tried to be halfway cordial. I'm sure he saw through me like a piece of plate glass.

The big blast came as we settled in the Chiefs' Mess for the evening movie. Dave LaRue and I were sitting together and finished laughing about the skunk in the Chiefs' barracks when the light went out and the movie started.

It was one of those movies that starts with an action scene then leads into the title. As the name of the star hit the screen the lights came on and the movie stopped. The place started filling up with Chiefs. Most were standing as five Chiefs stood in front of the screen and waited.

When the place quieted, one of them spoke.

"We've had an incident arise that has caused some dissension. I'm not going to say who, what, when, or where. Some of you already know about it so we'll leave it at that. Now let's hear what these men have to say."

Every one of them said their piece. Each had a different topic. We went through naval history and tradition. These were speeches of the roll and importance of Chief Petty Officers to the Navy. Before they finished their speeches, I knew what the problem was and who caused it.

Me!

When everything finished ninety to ninety-five percent of the Chiefs were in agreement. It was in fact, a conspiracy to commit mutiny. It was not a mutiny to take command of a vessel, but rather a renewal or refresher course in the literal power of the CPO's.

I thought to myself, "What have I done?"

Chapter 23

The next three days of ORI were miserable in two ways. First, it was long and tedious . . . drill after drill and flight OPS seemed to never cease. Second, it was a screwed up mess . . . nothing went right.

Planes were grounded because of lack of repair parts. The Avionics Department couldn't seem to get any COM/NAV gear in an up status. There was no need for the helicopters to try ASW operations without their dipping sonar. For those planes that did make it off, their communications with the ship had to be constantly repeated. The planes in the air that tried to land had more wave offs than they had ever encountered.

The ship's maneuverability was sluggish, and it had difficulty turning into the wind. Food handling equipment was always faulty and meals were never on time and tasted worse. Sickbay became swamped with more cases than they dreamed possible. Laundry services crashed, and hot water throughout the ships became almost nonexistent.

General Quarters no longer took less than four minutes. Each time it sounded, it took close to ten minutes to set condition ZEBRA. Once when GQ was supposed to be sounded, the alarm system wouldn't work at all. Only a few people on or about the bridge and in the Combat Information Center knew anything about it.

It was during the afternoon of our second day the scuttlebutt was received of conversations in the Officers' Wardroom. They were complaining of their food and personal service.

The ship's Boatswain, a Chief Warrant Officer, was overheard to have said, "I seen a situation like this back in WW II. At that time it seemed as though some Ltjg. or Ensign were about to swing at some Chief Petty Officers aboard the Cincinnati. We were the only cruiser operating off the coast of Manila, and not long before that we'd received a few ninety-day wonders as replacements. They came aboard knowing everything there was to know about the Navy.

"I was a Seaman First at the time. It was this full fleet Ensign that took over the First Division and tried to tell the Chief Boatswain Mate how things were to be done. Old Chief McMurtry . . . I'll never forget that guy. Nevertheless, he didn't go for it, and it didn't take long for those two to create one great big mess. Never thought I'd ever see that come about again. Sure seems similar to this mess. Yes sir, it takes quite a bit of organization for a ship to completely fall apart like this. Never thought it possible for a vessel this large.

"You guys wouldn't know anything about some Ensign and a Chief getting cross threaded on this bucket? Maybe it was a Jg. or a Lieutenant? Sometimes it takes three or four years before it sinks into the heads of these college grads. Those who learn first and fast seem to have smooth sailing. It doesn't happen to Mustangs . . . got to be some Joe college grad."

When I heard about it, I thought, "That old boatswain wasn't born yesterday. I bet if that guy and I even had a casual conversation he'd know in a minute."

We got the bottom line as we returned to Hawaii. We were operating off the coast when the ORI inspectors were flown back to Pearl. Within the hour after the last was gone, the 1MC came on, "Attention. Attention All Hands." There were a few unusual squeaks and pops then, "This is the captain speaking. This has been, without doubt, the worst exercise I have ever been in during my naval career. Never before, as a Division Officer, as a Department Head, or Commanding Officer have I been so embarrassed and so humiliated. We have failed our inspection.

"This does not take us out of the lineup for WestPac. It only delays it a few days.

"The squadrons that have joined us have worked hard to meet their commitments. For the next few days they will be sitting this one out.

"I can assure you this ship will get straightened out, then we will invite them to rejoin us. All of you can visualize and better anticipate what the next three days are going to be like. That is all."

That evening there was a message sent to the XO canceling his Temporary Additional Orders and telling him to return to the ship immediately.

We spent most of that day and a half with drill after drill and most of the crew become irritable. Fights were easily started and there were lots of pushes and shoves.

Within twenty-four hours of his message the XO was back on board and the Captain flew to Pearl for a conference with CinCPacFlt.

It was about 8:30 in the morning when Chief LaRue came into my office. He said, "I think you and I had better have a talk."

We stepped out the door into the passageway, and he said, "They're on to you like stink on you-know-what. I just got called into the squadron commander's office. It seems as though your Exec had one very exciting department meeting last night. I didn't say a thing, but that XO of yours has got your number. Just figured I'd warn you, old buddy."

I asked, "Just how did he find out? Somebody has fingered me, haven't they?"

He replied, "I've no idea. I've told you all I know."

I gave him my thanks. He went into the shop, and I went back into the office.

Lieutenant Carter said, "The XO wants to see you in his cabin right now. He didn't sound happy."

I knew something was definitely wrong. I asked myself, "What is going on?"

When I got to his cabin, the marine guard was standing at parade rest facing forward. He eyed me, and when I was within speaking distance, he said I was to have a seat and the XO would see me shortly.

My heart was beating at a miserable pace, and I could have used some of Doc Swanson's liquid. I knew I was going to get killed. The end was in sight.

I waited.

There was a slight sound of the doorknob, and the marine snapped to attention. I did likewise. We were two boards when Lieutenant Harcourt came out of the cabin.

He gave me a "kill" look as he passed by. I dared not smile.

"Wilson!"

I knew I had less than one minute to live. I was so stiff I would have put that marine to shame as far as standing at attention goes.

I was shocked when he said, "Chief, I'm just as easy going as anybody you'll ever meet. Have a seat. Relax."

I was going to live for at least one more minute.

I sat down, but I never relaxed. I was still terrified.

He continued, "Didn't take me long to track down this mess between you and Harcourt. I told him just as I'm telling you. It ends here. It ends now."

He walked around his desk and sat down. He grinned a little and said, "See how simple this is?"

His grin crashed! "You keep away from Harcourt. You go start making phone calls and tell all those Chiefs it's over. You have twelve hours. We are going to stand down from all drills, the men will have time to relax, eat, and get a few hours sleep. Showers will be made available with hot water. The time they have will depend on how fast you and the grapevine operates.

"You can also let it be known that at precisely 2200 there will be a GQ and this ship will be buttoned down in less than four minutes.

"I don't think I would even be amazed by how many aircraft are repaired and back in an up status within that period. I would even go as far as to say that this ship will be able to turn on a dime. You are following me, aren't you, Chief?"

"Yes, sir."

"Now to make myself perfectly clear, get out of here, and I don't want to hear another word. Don't even say, 'Yes sir.' Get out!"

Once again, as my hand touched the doorknob, I heard the marine guard snap to attention. His heels cracked and it echoed down through the passageway.

It was strange. I went straight to the Chiefs' Mess, and the place was crowded. I think I was expected.

All eyes were upon me. I said, "It's all over. We lost and the XO won."

There were some "I'm glads," some "It's about times," and other indistinguishable mumbling.

I still had center stage. "The way it was put to me is that the aircraft will be in an up status, this ship will turn on a dime, and there will be GQ at 2200. The ship will set Zebra in less than four minutes. There will be hot showers, good food, and rest until then. There were no ifs, ands, buts, or maybes. I was allowed to say 'yes sir' one time. That was when he said, 'Do I make myself clear?'"

From somewhere in the crowd someone shouted, "We never lost!" He worked his way to where I was standing. It was a Chief Machinist Mate. He said, "I don't ever want to hear that a Chief Petty Officer lost.

"We won! We have shown every one who really runs this man's Navy. We've never doubted, now they don't."

He looked at me and said, "And you, Jack Wilson, an E-8 saying such a thing. I don't ever want to hear you say we lost." He looked around and spoke to the crowd, "I don't ever want to hear that from anybody. Is that clear?

"We, the Chiefs, took this ship apart in less than twelve hours and we, the Chiefs, can put it back together in less than twelve hours.

"Now let's get out of here and do it. We have work to do."

The mess cleared out. The cooks were busy preparing lunch, and the mess cooks were hurriedly setting the table. I looked up and Dave LaRue was standing in front of me.

We walked up the ladder and across the hangar deck. He put his arm around my shoulders and said, "Old buddy, I think we just went through another one and believe me, and I'm surprised you're still alive."

We laughed as we walked to the Avionics Shop. When we entered, the men were already putting tags on equipment they repaired some time back. I was surprised when someone said, "We tried."

I smiled a little then Chief Hawkins said, "All right you guys, get that gear down to the squadrons. Volunteer to help in swapping out that stuff. Find out what it's like to work on the line. You're not going to be on the bench all your life."

Chief LaRue said, "That goes for you VA boys also. Let's get a move on it."

I looked at the Third Class who said, "We tried" and I said, "No, we didn't just try. We, and I do mean we, did it."

Chapter 24

There was still the matter of Baker to be settled. I had not accomplished anything in his behalf.

The ORI went with excellent marks on everything. It was said that it was one of the smoothest operations ever graded.

The XO had put off all masts until it was completed. We were now on our way to the Gulf of Tonkin, and we knew it. We had one stop to make before going on station. Subic Bay. We were near Wake Island when I got another call to report to the executive officer's cabin.

Jeez. I'd been good and so had Martin. Baker wasn't speaking to me, but I didn't care. As far as I knew everything was going fine. Since ORI every day had been a basic eight-hour workday.

Again as I approached the Executive Officer's cabin, the same marine guard was standing at parade rest near the entrance. He nodded toward the chair so I made myself comfortable for what I could. I squirmed for a while then again the marine clicked his heels and snapped to attention. I stood.

It was Lieutenant Harcourt who came out. He pulled the door closed behind him and glared at me.

He said, "You got me transferred as Unsuitable Personnel. You're the one that caused this."

In his same tone I answered him, "Unsuitable Personnel. Believable."

"Wilson, you've ruined my naval career!"

"Lieutenant, with your attitude, you never had a naval career!"

He drew back for a swing. In the same instant there was a clicking of the heels and a shout, "T Hut!"

The echo of his heels hadn't ceased before the three of us were at attention. When Lieutenant Harcourt looked around only the three of us were still present.

The Lieutenant stormed off.

The marine looked at me and winked. That was the closest thing I had to a relaxing moment in the last thirty minutes.

The XO called me in.

"So this is all about one lousy barroom brawl. Don't you think I know how to handle these things? Give me a little credit. Chief, I've told you life can be simple, but you don't want to listen to me. I've seen to it that Harcourt is out of my hair, but you you're something else. I have to go through BuPers to get you out of my hair. I don't have to put up with you around the Wardroom so I'm going to keep you around for a while. The Maintenance Officer has put in a good word for you, but you can thank your lucky stars that you're not in the Administration Department.

"I've dismissed all the cases that Lieutenant Harcourt has been working on. I want to start with a clean sheet in the Legal Department. Legal Officers are easier to come by than good Avionics Chiefs. I've got a bargain for you. You run your Avionics Shop, and I'll run the ship. How does that sound?"

I started to speak, but he raised his hand like a traffic cop and said, "I don't want to hear it. See how simple things can be? Now get out!" His last words were quite strong.

I left his office, and as I walked out the door the marine was at attention. I closed the door to the cabin and mumbled an audible, "Thanks."

I went to the Chiefs' Mess to have a couple cups of coffee and quit shaking so much. From there I went to the AIMD berthing compartment and found Baker.

"You're completely off the hook. I just came from the Executive Officer's cabin, and he told me everything that Lieutenant Harcourt had ready for mast has been thrown in the trash." I left Baker and never heard a word out of him.

I thought, "See how easy things can be . . . Right!"

I climbed the ladders back to my office. Dave LaRue was waiting outside the office door.

He said, "Lieutenant Harcourt has packed his belonging and is waiting in the Ready Room. He's taking the COD to Wake Island. From there he's catching a flight to the States. His orders are to Norfolk.

"Thought you'd like to know."

"I'll swear you've got more eyes and ears than anyone I've ever ran across. You know, he even tried to take a swing at me."

"Knew that too. Want to go up and wave to him as he gets on the COD?"

I said, "Why not? Just to twist the knife a little."

Dave and I went together up to the flight deck. Our timing was perfect. He leaned back against the superstructure and I was about twenty feet out in the open and aft of the plane when the Lt. walked toward the COD.

I whistled real loud and gave him the one finger bird.

He looked at me then acted as if to ignore me.

We went back into the superstructure and started down. He was leading the way so I yelled, "Let's hit your locker. I think we have a toast to make."

He laughed.

We went to the Chiefs' berthing area where LaRue and I made a toast or two to Lt. Harcourt. Well, it may have been three or four toasts. Maybe more, I forgot.

The next morning let me know that it may have been five or six. I slept in. It was near 0830 when I got up. By the time I showered, dressed, and had a cup (or two) of coffee in me it was near 0945 when I reached my office.

Martin said that Master Chief Madson wanted to see me just as soon as I showed up. When he said Master Chief Madson, I knew I was in for it again. As I left my office, I said to myself, "I've been good. I'll swear I've been good."

As I got to his office he said, "Come on in, Jack. Close the door behind you."

(Once again I thought, "I've been good.")

"How long have you known Chief LaRue?"

"It seems like all of my life. Seventeen, maybe eighteen years. I met him at AT "A" school in Memphis. Why?"

"Just curious. Was he recently in Traverse City, Michigan?"

"Yes. Why?"

"Did he ever mention to you what he was doing there?"

"He said he was on recruiting duty."

"Do you know of any relationship between him and our Executive Officer? Or why he seems to frequently visit with the Executive Officer?"

"No! What's going on here?"

"Oh, nothing. One of my men in the mechanic shop said that he swore he met him in Traverse City, that's all. Now let's tackle the next subject. Did you and he happen to meet Mr. Jack Daniels last night?"

Now I knew what it was about, but I didn't understand about LaRue and the XO.

"Yes, we did."

"As the Leading Chief of this outfit, I do make it my business to know what is going on around here. You know good and well liquor is not allowed aboard ship. We both know there is a lot of that stuff in and around the Chiefs. It's actions like yours that spread the word around in places . . ."

He cut himself short. "Jack, I'll tell you now. I've always kind of liked you. I know you'll be looking toward E-9 soon, and I've met Dr. Swanson. Don't let this screw you up in any manner or method. You will be up at 0600 tomorrow morning won't you?"

"Yes."

"That's all I have unless you'd like a few aspirins or maybe another cup of coffee."

"No, thanks. That is, no to the aspirins and coffee and the thanks is just for . . . well, thanks."

Chapter 25

Martin was doing his job as I expected and paid very little attention to him. Frequently, in the evenings I went back to my office, and he would be writing letters or reading books. He and the Chaplain's assistant, who ran the library, became close friends and spent lots of time together.

However there are certain things young men have to explore, and Martin got his first taste when we hit Subic Bay.

I thought we had a full load of ammunition before we left the States, but we spent most of our time at Subic taking on more ammunition. I didn't think the bombs would ever stop being loaded and Martin knew they wouldn't. He got his first taste of an All Hands working party.

After the stores were loaded, liberty was granted to those who were not on watch. Martin and I headed for town.

Even though Dave and I spent a lot of time together, he declined an invitation to go with Martin and I. I never heard a bad word from him about Martin and like this time he said, "I'll pass."

Jim and I hit one of the lowest level joints I could find. I had one more lesson I wanted him to learn before I considered him weaned. I knew he'd never been around anything like this.

As we sat in a booth, one of the young hostesses sat next to Jim. She asked for him to buy her a drink. I nodded my approval. She had a drink delivered, and I watched as Jim's eyes started to glaze over and his breathing became erratic.

I interrupted, "Feels good doesn't it? Now just what would you think if some young guy was rubbing Janet's leg like that?"

It hit home! Again I thought someone wanted to take a swing at me. Before he spoke I continued, "It's a two way street. Think about it."

I watched him close as he told the girl to leave. She said a few words of an undesirable nature and some in the language of the Philippines.

I asked, "Want to leave?"

We left our drinks sitting on the table and started a little window-shopping. We discussed prices and then started looking for a bar with a little class. It took a few looks inside, but we finally found one. One that wasn't smoke filled, one with very few hostesses, and one with fans to cool the sweat.

Again I gave him $200 and said, "You may need that to buy more presents. Keep Janet in the front of your mind at all times. We still have a long way to go."

He answered, "The way you put it to me, I will keep Janet, and her leg, in my mind."

We finished our beer, and I left him to do his shopping. I thought he could learn a lot on his own. He's going to have to learn to sink or swim according to his decisions.

These past couple of weeks hadn't done my ulcers much good, but at the moment I was feeling good.

I found myself another bar and was enjoying the silence when I heard, "Well, old buddy, I thought I'd be able to find you. Trying to drown your ulcers huh?"

"Dave. You do have instincts I never suspected."

I ordered us a couple more beers. I finished the one I had and reached for the second. Another hand beat me to it.

I looked up. It was Doc Swanson.

I immediately thought of how my mother used to scold me.

He said, "Chief, I've tried to tell you. You just won't listen will you? I don't want to cut you open any more than you. I don't think Doris would like it very much either.

"Second thought, don't think of your ulcers, don't think of yourself and above all, don't think about Doris. Let me tattoo my initials across your stomach."

He set my beer back down in front of me. When he said, 'Don't think about Doris,' I thought of what I had just told Jim. Think about Janet.

I even thought about that XO. Life can be so simple.

"Well Dave, the world's against me. Got to give it up. You've got two." I slid the beer over to him and reached in my pocket and from the roll of antacid I extracted a tablet and popped it into my mouth. I made a terrible face and said, "Mmmm, these are sooo good."

The weather had been good to us. The day after we left Subic Bay we ran into some rain and choppy seas. Of course, that was the day that we refueled at sea.

Martin and I watched. He got his pictures, himself quite wet, and a little seasick.

I could tell it didn't bother those old boys on the tanker as much as it did our men, but that's the way it goes. Other than that it was just the sun and us.

We made it through our first tour on Yankee Station with little incident. We had a couple of F8 photo planes to land that had bullet holes in them. They belonged to the Kitty Hawk, but came to us for fuel and were catapulted off immediately after refueling. Our A4's were flying high and unloading bombs faster than the Ordnancemen could load them.

We left Vietnam and spent a week in Yokosuka, Japan. Jim and I spent a day in Tokyo. It was all sight seeing and spending money. Jim tried all the foods and found he liked some. Of course, he tried his hand at chopsticks and sake. He didn't care much for the hot sake, but became proficient in the use of chopsticks . . . for a round eye. Doc Swanson had definitely come between the bottle and me. At least, he put Doris in there somewhere.

We went back to Vietnam for a second go, but never went north of Da Nang.

We were off the coast of the southern tip near Saigon when Martin came into the office. It was still early evening and the air conditioning was better than what Southeast Asia offered.

"Chief, do you remember me telling you about the disbursing clerk a few months ago?"

"Yeh, what about it?"

"He was sitting across the mess deck from me. There was a table between us, but I kept feeling his eyes on me. You know the feeling. Anyhow, I looked up at him a few times and noticed that he was watching me. He acted strange."

"So?"

"So nothing. Just thought it was very strange."

"You haven't mentioned Whitteker in some time. Are you two getting along all right?"

"Sure. Good friends. We see each other every so often. I'm spending more and more time in the library and just don't wander around skylarking as much as I used to."

"Any other particular reason you came up here?"

"Just to write a letter. We'll be heading back soon and I wanted to get a letter off before it was too late."

"Malarkey. The mail plane leaves here every day. We've got lots of time for writing letters."

"I wanted to tell you about the disbursing clerk."

"Bull! You're beating around the bush. You're stammering too much."

"I knew you'd be here. I want to say thanks while I have the opportunity and with no one else around. Thanks for bringing me. It has been an experience."

I said, "You can say that again."

"I hope I haven't been too much trouble."

"We're not home free. Still got a few weeks to go. We'll celebrate when we get home. If you're starting to get soft on me, I'm leaving."

I closed the door behind me, walked around a while and went to the Chief's Quarters, showered, and hit the sack early.

It was near 9 AM when I got another phone call. I answered, "Chief Wilson speaking, sir."

"Strike three, Chief Wilson. Would you care to join me in my dugout?"

It can only be imagined what I shouted.

I overheard what the XO said. "If you think he could possibly help you, do bring him along."

The sound on the phone changed to a dial tone.

Once again the same marine guard was standing by the door of the Executive Officer's cabin. He opened the door for me, and with my hat in my hand, I went right in.

It was terrible. I stood at attention during the complete dissertation. I was to be shot at sunrise. I was to be hanged at high noon. I was to sit in the electric chair at midnight. While I was there, I dared not breath.

When he got through with me, I went to the Chiefs' Mess. My legs ached from standing at attention. My knees were sore from knocking. My blood pressure was either below 50 or above 200, I couldn't tell which.

I was shaking so much I spilled my coffee over into the saucer. I was too weak to bring it to my lips. It was terrible.

"Well old buddy, you and the Exec had another chat, huh?"

"For crying out loud Dave, is there anything that goes on around here that you don't know about?"

"Not very much. Oh, by the way, there's always good news on the horizon. Here's a telegram for you. Doris won another golf tournament. She didn't come in second here like she did at Pebble Beach. She took first place on this one."

"LaRue! You even read my mail."

"Not me, old buddy. Just happen to be in the radio shack when it came it. Ease up a bit. Is the old man going to have you drawn and quartered? Maybe keel hauled?"

I answered, "All of the above," as I managed to get a sip of coffee down.

"Tell old Dave what's it all about. It isn't still over that kid of yours is it?"

"What do you mean that kid of mine?" My expression must have drastically changed.

"That kid, Martin. You know what I mean."

Again my heart leaped into my throat. "What do you mean Martin?"

"Come on, Jack. Everybody knows you're the good old boy that went to bat for him over the ruckus in the bar."

Again my expression changed for I didn't know what he was talking about. For a moment I thought he was talking about Martin being a stowaway. He must have sensed my ignorance.

"Jack, are you honestly that naive?" He looked at me and said, "You never knew that it was Martin that started the fight in the bar? It wasn't Baker, your PPO. Man, he was sitting in there minding his own business. He's the one that was holding some dude onto the floor with a bar stool when the cops came in."

"No, I never knew."

"It was those two yo-yo's that got Martin out of there while Baker held him captive. That's when the three of them came in where we were and Martin poured the beer on me."

I was in a daze.

"You do remember that part don't you? Your brain isn't as fried as your stomach is it?"

"Yeh, I remember that part. The other, honestly I never knew."

"Everyone else did. That Lieutenant was such an idiot he didn't know that we take care of our own. That's part of why everybody on board backed you up. When the smoke cleared, that Martin has sure cost Uncle Sam a lot of money and has caused the whole crew of the ship a lot of grief, hard work, and long hours.

"Well old buddy, now I want to know. Is it all over, and is he worth it?"

"It's all over, Dave, and I sure hope the kid is worth it."

I never mentioned anything to Martin about the bar incident, and I never spoke to ADJ3 Baker. I can see now that "You owe me one Chief." I sure did.

We made one last stop in Yokosuka. I knew it was the end of the line for Jim Martin AZAN so we spent a lot of money and did a lot of sightseeing.

We were tied up starboard side, and I was standing in the starboard catwalk when I heard over the 1MC, "The Officer-of-the-Deck is shifting his watch from the Quarter-deck to the Bridge." I checked my watch. Everything seemed to be on time. It was exactly on time as it should be.

I looked out across the shipyard for somehow I knew this would be my last look at Japan.

Again the 1MC blurted, "The ship is underway. The ship is underway."

Music immediately followed:

CALIFORNIA HERE I COME!

Chapter 26

While we were in Yokosuka, I had three wooden plaques made. They were identical in the shape of a shield. Two were about four inches across with a small brass plate with engraving that read, "THANKS" and in smaller letters it said "ATCS Jack Wilson."

The third plaque was larger and had three military medals mounted on its face. The medals were the NATIONAL DEFENSE, REPUBLIC OF VIET-NAM SERVICE, and a medal from the country of VIET NAM. Below the medals was a small brass plate that read, "AZAN JAMES L. MARTIN, UNITED STATES NAVY."

The day before we pulled into San Diego I gave the two small plaques to Gray and Whitteker and the larger one to Martin.

Whitteker gave me his thanks and said, "Chief, you had to have been out of your mind to even think of trying to pull this off."

Gray shook his head and said, "I'd never have believed it."

My reply to this was, "I knew *we* could do it."

When we pulled in, it was full dress whites and flight deck parade as we rounded Point Loma. Shortly thereafter, upon dismissal, it was a free for all.

Jim ran to his compartment and retrieved his camera. He met me at a predetermined spot.

Almost all hands were either on the flight deck, in the catwalks, on the hangar deck or standing on the sponsons. That's where Jim and I were. Once again he was putting his camera to use.

Anxiety was rampant throughout the ship.

Our guests who said good-bye to us six months ago were here to greet us as we came in.

Doris and I were as close as we could be with her on the pier and me on the sponson. We just looked at each other as the men created a mob at the afterbrow waiting for a chance to leave.

As soon as the afterbrow was set, Jim was off the ship in a flash. He must have beaten me to the pier by several hundred people. By the time I greeted our guests, Jim had already received hugs and kisses from everyone. Doris even gave him a big kiss.

Jim's mouth was running a mile a minute talking to Janet.

Just about the only thing Paul could say was, "You're crazy, you did it."

I didn't mind being called crazy . . . and only a fool would have tried.

Once the crowd thinned out, we went aboard and carried our packages off the ship. Jim and I made a couple more trips back to the ship while the others stayed at their cars. We loaded all the gifts we had bought.

With that task finished, we went to the Martin's house. While Dolly, Doris, Paul, and I talked, Jim and Janet disappeared.

After we had a sandwich, Doris and I decided to go to Long Beach. It was on the way home that she told me we had to return to San Diego that evening.

I didn't mind the round trip, but I did want to get home and do a little catching up. As Jim and Janet, we too needed a little privacy.

Doris and I returned to San Diego and arrived at the Hotel Del Coronado promptly at 8 PM. I thought something had gotten out of hand when Gray, Whitteker, Jim and Janet and Mr. and Mrs. Martin greeted us. Everyone was dressed for the occasion. We had spoken of having a get together to celebrate the accomplishment of my hoax.

Yes, my hoax. I conceived the idea and formulated the plans. Certainly I had to have collaborators, coordinators, co-operators, co-conspirators, or whatever names you wish to choose, but the idea was still mine. Nevertheless we had considered a party, but I had not put this one together.

It was Doris who told me that we were to meet Paul and Dolly at the hotel promptly at 8:00. She did not say who told her, but said she understood they had reservations and we were to dress for the occasion. After all, it was The Hotel Del Coronado.

Gray, Whitteker, and all were in dress clothes. I had never visualized these guys in ties? The thought never occurred to me. They looked quite nice. Nobody claimed credit for the execution of this gathering, however it was unimportant at this time. We entered as a group not knowing exactly what to expect next. As we approached the Maitre D,' he greeted us with, "Mr. Wilson, your table is this way."

Wait just a minute. Why was the table in my name? I had not made reservation. Maybe Doris had. Maybe she had been pulling my leg, and this was her welcome home gift and celebration.

Again nobody claimed credit so I decided to go along. It will all come to light in due time.

We ordered our drinks. While I was trying to get my thoughts together the others introduced themselves around. Jim was the only person other than myself who knew Gray and Whitteker. These two guys were looking Janet over quite thoroughly when our drinks arrived. The drinks consisting of coffee, cola, and marguerites, were distributed by order and of course, age.

Just about the time I decided to start inquiring about the gathering an unexpected guest interrupted us.

"Good evening. Allow me to introduce myself. I am Commander Alexander, the Executive Officer of the USS Kreighton."

"I know who each of you are and now, you know who I am."

He pulled up a chair and sat down.

"With respect to the civilians at the table, I am going to ask you not to say a word until after I leave the table. With respect from the military at the table, I am telling you to keep your mouth shut until I leave the table. I have asked the waiter not to take your order until I leave.

"Now that I know we will not be disturbed. I'll get to the point. I am the one who called this meeting, and I will have the floor, without interruption.

"First, I know all that transpired in this past year. After I unraveled this mess, I decided to ride it out rather than make a mess of an undesirable situation. Now that it's over, I want it finished. Completely and entirely finished. I don't want a single word of this fiasco to get out of this room.

Not one single word. I'll swear to goodness that if I ever hear anything similar to a sea story about this I am going to start killing people."

It seemed the more he talked, the louder his voice got and the redder his face got.

"Just what the world do you people think?" He realized he had asked a question and cut himself short. Not only that, he was beginning to rise from his seat.

Now I knew of his mood. I'd seen him this angry before.

He sat back down. Took a deep breath, tried to relax, and started again.

"You," he said as he glared and pointed to Jim. "I want you to put a liberty card, a Geneva Convention card, and an ID card on the table in front of you. No, I want you to hold them in your hand, fanned out like a poker hand and just hold them there for all to see. Keep them there until I ask for them."

Upon this order, Jim proceeded to do exactly as instructed.

After he spoke to Jim, the Commander reached down beside him and opened a briefcase. I noted it was one of the old types that have a strap across the top with a single latch. It must have been military issue. However, that is of no importance.

From the briefcase he pulled out a large white envelope marked "OFFICIAL DOCUMENT" and it had the name Whitteker written on it.

"You, young man," he said as he looked straight at Whitteker, "have let it be known in no uncertain terms about how you have wanted to get out of this canoe club. Well, here it is. Effective tomorrow you are being honorably discharged from the United States Navy. You are getting a three-month cut and if you ever decide to re-enlist, don't do it around here or around me.

"And you," he said as he turned to Gray. Again he reached into the briefcase and came up with another white "OFFICIAL DOCUMENT" envelope. "Effective tomorrow, you are being transferred to Aviation Electronic Technician school at Memphis. When you leave there, God help you if you ever show up at any duty station in which I am involved.

"At 0700 tomorrow morning you two will report to your respective department offices. There two marine guards will meet you. You will not be allowed to speak to anyone. You will enter and pack your personal belongings. From there you will be escorted to your berthing compartment. There you will pack all your belongings. The marines will see to this, and they will also help you carry your gear to the afterbrow. Next, you will be escorted to the Disbursing Office. The disbursing officer will be there.

"You will be given all the pay and allowances that is presently on the books. You will also receive all monies required for you to carry out these orders. This will all be accomplished by 0900.

"From there you will be escorted back to the afterbrow. You and your gear will depart the ship. You will not be allowed back aboard. The Chief of the Watch has his orders.

"Now you." He looked me straight in the eyes. "You are going to get a little more slack. I've had two cruise boxes built for you. Four marines will be waiting for you at the entrance to the Chiefs' Mess at 0800. They will assist you in packing your gear in the Chiefs' Quarters and in the Avionics Office. You too, are instructed to speak to no one. Greetings and salutations are accepted . . . nothing more. The mess treasurer will have your shares waiting for you.

"After your gear is packed, the marines will carry your gear off the ship and deposit it at the bottom of the gangplank. Arrangements from there are your responsibility.

"If any of you think you are being treated as common criminals, I don't think you want to bring any complaints to my attention."

Once more he reached into the briefcase. Another envelope. Sure enough it was marked "Wilson."

"You are being temporarily transferred to the US Naval Air Station, North Island, California. There you will make necessary travel arrangements for your ultimate duty station, NAS, Atsugi, Japan."

Believe me, Doris and I were astonished. We looked at each other and were sure that the other was going to have a heart attack.

"You with the cards in your hands are the last. I effectively have no control over you. I will have two marines to meet you at the afterbrow. They will escort you to your berthing space where you will pack your belongings. From there you will be escorted to the afterbrow where you will deposit these items. From there you will be escorted to your division office where you will gather the remainder of your belongings.

"As I said, I have no control over you. However, I suggest that you not say a word to the marines and have mercy on your soul if you give them any static.

"Just nod your head if you are receiving the intent of what I'm saying."

Jim nodded affirmatively.

"I ran a security check on you. I have a copy of your school records. I know your mother and father want you to go to college. Your scholastic standing has indicated you should continue your education."

He paused shortly.

"Punishment?" he seemed to question.

"I cannot punish you by any means or manner. However, there are other methods of reprisal. I understand you and the young lady have intentions of being married. Maybe I can interfere with this enough to open her eyes or make the wait worth while."

We had all sat there dumbfounded and, as instructed, had not said a word. When he said this, Janet made a move as if she was about to stand and open her mouth. Luckily, I was sitting beside her. As she moved, I grasped her left arm and reassured her of her seat.

The Commander continued speaking to Jim, "I have stated that I cannot punish you. There are others that can. Upperclassmen. I have procured by the best means possible, my brother, Senator Alexander, an appointment for you to the Naval Academy at Annapolis. The upperclassmen will, as necessary, take care of that end, and if you should decide to take this appointment, you will be prohibited from getting married for five years. One year of prep school and four more years until graduation. That's all that I can do."

He turned to Janet and said, "Sorry, young lady."

He then retrieved another white envelope. He handed it to Jim and firmly grasped the three cards Jim had been holding.

The Commander stood up, fastened his briefcase, reached inside his coat pocket, and handed me another piece of paper. "This is the check for my meal. Take care of it for me, Chief.

"I caution each and every one of you, not one word. Tonight. Tomorrow. Forever. Not one word."

For some reason, maybe egotistical, I got the feeling that he admired our intestinal fortitude. That is in the conceiving and execution of the plan. However, I'm sure he didn't like the idea of it happening within his command.

After he walked away from the table, we all broke loose. We were ecstatic. We had all received exactly what we wanted, and he was getting rid of a handful of pests.

I stood up, and again I raised my right arm with a clinched fist and shouted, "I got even! No, I won. *I won!*"

Not one word? Not one word!

I'm going to write a book.

What ever happened to old what's-his-name?

When we split up, we swore to each other we would stay in touch. This went over for a while and after about a year it dwindled to nothing.

Whitteker bummed around on his motorcycle for a while and later went to visit Gray at the Naval Air Station just outside of Memphis. It was during this visit he was killed when his motorcycle tangled with an automobile.

Aviation Electronics Technician Third Class Gray finished his school and was transferred to NAS Oceana, Virginia.

Jim Martin went to the Naval Academy. Stories were that he had previous military experience and was made the Master at Arms of his dorm. He wrote to me and told me how many times he thought of Baker, the PPO aboard the Kreighton.

His heart problem was missed on his first physical. It was after he finished prep school that they found it. He was discharged at the convenience of the government for pre-existing conditions.

It didn't work out too bad for him. He became entitled to the GI Bill of Rights for his college tuition. He and Janet got married, and after two years away from Mom and Dad he didn't want to stay in San Diego. They moved to San Jose where he is finishing his studies at San Jose State.

Mr. and Mrs. Martin are living a life that I classify as good citizens. Nothing exciting. Just an eight to five job at Convair.

Chief David LaRue flew off the ship on the last COD flight as we were coming back to the States. After he left the ship, Chief Madson and I had another short conversation concerning Dave. It seems as though the airman in the mechanic shop knew him as Lieutenant LaRue. It also turned out that Chief Madson's brother is an FBI agent. He located a David LaRue that works for Naval Intelligence. The Chief made it quite clear that it was one and the same Dave LaRue. I've never heard from or about him since.

It's an "I spy," "You spy," "Nobody knows a thing" world.

Doris and I finished our tour of duty at Atsugi. We enjoyed it as much as we had anticipated. I retired from the service there.

On our way back home we passed through San Diego and visited with the Martins for a couple of days. We had a lot of good laughs.

One in particular we repeated over and over. As a matter of fact the more Paul and I drank, the more we said, "Not one word!" I never realized how many ways that it could be said. A whisper. A shout. No matter how we said it, we laughed as we had never laughed before.

Oh well, so much for that.

Doris works at the golf course during the summer months, but no longer participates in tournaments. Her three-year idle time in Japan took the sharpness off her game. She did play some. They have some nice golf courses in Japan, but I never embarrassed her by playing there.

I am now selling Buicks for my father-in-law. What an exciting life . . .

Yes, I, ATCM Jack B. Wilson, United States Navy, Re-tired, did write the book.

Oh, it's title . . . ?

"Jack Wilson, Chief Petty Officer, USN"

THE END

I hope you enjoyed reading the novel as much as I en-joyed writing it.

Leon R. Shafer

To order additional copies of

JACK WILSON
Chief Petty Officer, U.S.N.

Please visit our web site at
www.pleasantword.com

Also available at: www.amazon.com

Printed in the United States
23754LVS00001B/148-195